THE VOW

MIA KENT

The Vow

By Mia Kent

Be the first to know about new releases! Sign up for my newsletter here. Your information will never be shared.

CHAPTER 1

At the sound of the bell chiming, Jax Keller dropped the knife he was holding, smoothed out his chef's apron, and headed for the inn's front door. When he reached it, he stopped with his hand on the doorknob, taking a moment to steady his nerves and flick a sprig of parsley from his palm before pulling it open with a smile.

"At your service," Daphne said with a grin and a curtsy as she stood before him in a crisp white shirt and black pants. "Do I look fancy enough? I didn't think those ridiculous fifties-style dresses Sal made the waitresses wear at the diner would be appropriate for tonight." She did a little twirl, and Jax couldn't help but admire the view—more than two decades may have passed since the last time he'd held her in his arms and stared deeply into those beautiful ocean-blues, but the years had somehow only made her more beautiful.

"You look great," he said, unable to hide the sincerity in his tone—and the longing, too. He realized he'd been holding his breath, and he let it out on a soft exhale, his eyes never leaving her face. His heart rate kicked up a notch, and it was only then that he realized most of the anxiety he'd been experiencing over the past few hours had little to do with Steve Neuman, the successful restaurant investor he was looking to impress, and everything to do with the woman standing before him.

Their gazes caught, and Jax tried to avert his eyes so she wouldn't see the truth written in them, but it was too late—she stopped mid-twirl, her expression hardening almost imperceptibly as she straightened up and smoothed down an invisible crease in her shirt before stepping through the door, giving him a wide berth so they wouldn't accidentally brush up against each other. What she thought would happen if they did, Jax didn't know, he thought, trying to cover up a snort of amusement. It wasn't as if he was going to tackle her to the floor and declare his undying love for her.

No, that would happen only in the privacy of his own head. The undying love part, that is.

"So have you heard from Steve at all?" Daphne asked, continuing down the inn's hallway into the kitchen. She stepped inside and set her bag on the ground, then looked around in amusement. "Wow, you've certainly been… busy."

Which was an understatement, of course. Jax hadn't been busy; he'd been absolutely *frenzied,* and the stained countertops, dirty pots and pans filling the double sink, and the heaps of ingredients piled on every available surface were testimony to how he had spent his past few hours. No one could say he was unprepared, and Jax had every intention of knocking Steve Neuman's socks clean off his feet from the very first bite.

"He should be here in fifteen minutes," Jax said, eyeing his watch before fixing Daphne with a dubious look. "Cutting it a little close, aren't you? I was starting to think I'd have to be both server and chef."

"You're right, I needed to brush up on my waitressing skills for your solo customer," she said playfully, reaching into her bag for a crisp white apron and wrapping it around her waist. "Good thing I don't have twenty-seven years of experience to fall back on." Then she caught his eye and smiled. "Sorry, I lost track of time. Things are down to the wire at the bakery, and I'm still trying to tie up some loose ends."

"I know, and thank you again for your help." Jax leaned toward her, considering a hug, and then thought better of it… helped along, of course, by the tension that nearly oozed from her body every time he got close. He settled for a brotherly pat on the shoulder instead. "Remember, as a thank you for tonight, I'm going to be at your beck and call day and night until the bakery's grand opening. Anything you need, I'm your man."

They both fell silent as the implications of those words settled over them, the unspoken meaning behind them, the shadows of the past that neither of them had ever quite been able to escape from. Jax opened his mouth to say something more, but Daphne beat him to the punch, saying in a playful voice that he could hear was strained slightly at the edges, "Don't worry, I'm going to put you to work the second the sun rises tomorrow. After this week's over, you're going to be so sick of seeing my face that you'll be thrilled to catch that plane to Miami Beach."

Miami Beach. Halfway across the country from

Dolphin Bay, the small island off the coast of Maine that Daphne—and currently Jax—called home. He'd never stepped foot in Florida, and now, if he played his cards right, he'd be leaving the island, and leaving her, to start a new life in a world of unknowns. Until this moment, it had always seemed like a vague prospect, a distant, slightly worrying possibility that he had always pushed into the furthest corners of his mind.

But… why?

He was prepared for this. He was prepared to show Steve Neuman that he wasn't only capable of doing the job properly, but he was *hungry* for it. Hungry to return to his glory days, when he'd run the kitchen of one of the most acclaimed restaurants in Philadelphia. Different city, different setting, but that didn't matter—Jax would be doing what he loved since he was a child.

He'd also loved something else since he was a child.

Daphne's hair covered her face as she bent over the pots simmering on the stove, inhaling deeply into each one before replacing the lid and moving on to the next. When she caught Jax watching her, she blushed and said, "Sorry, I didn't have a chance to grab a bite before I came over here. Everything smells delicious." She stepped away from the stovetop, but Jax stopped her with a hand on her arm.

"Here, I made plenty—enough for twenty Steve Neumans." He dipped a spoon into the nearest pot and held it out to her. "Go on, have a taste. I'm a bundle of nerves right now—I could use a little ego-stroking."

"Well, then, I'm happy to oblige," Daphne said, taking the spoon and then adding, "Not that you need a bigger ego," with a wink. She brought the spoon to her lips, blowing on it before tasting the sauce that had been simmering for hours. "Oh my, Jax… this is delicious." She lowered the spoon with a shake of her head. "Is that…?"

"Rosemary mustard barbecue sauce. For these." He indicated a plate of ribs covered with aluminum foil; he'd spent the past few hours grilling them to perfection. "It's a bistro, so I decided to go with American-style food: ribs, burgers, pulled pork sandwiches, things like that."

"Stop. Please." Daphne pressed a hand to her stomach and moaned. "I can't take it anymore; that all sounds so incredible." She surveyed the dishes, hands on hips. "You're going to blow that restaurant investor's mind with the first bite."

"Let's hope so," Jax said, feeling a ball of nerves

forming in his stomach at the reminder. He glanced at the clock; Steve should be here in—

The inn's front door chimed again, and Jax straightened up, staring down the hallway, his heart pounding in his ears. This was it.

The time had come to show Steve Neuman what he was made of.

He headed for the kitchen entrance, but Daphne grabbed him by the arm and swung him around. "What are you doing?" she scolded, directing him back to the stove. "Since when have you gone into a restaurant and been greeted by the chef? I'll answer the door and get him settled; you focus on this." She waved her hand around to indicate the various unfinished platters of food scattered around the room, then made a beeline for the front door before Jax could give her a grateful smile.

Now alone, he ran his fingers through his hair, then braced his hands against the counter, white-knuckling the marble as he took three deep breaths and let them out slowly. In the distance, he could hear Daphne greeting Steve, followed by the sound of the man's booming voice growing closer as she led him into the dining room. Within moments, he would be seated with a glass of red wine and a napkin draped across his lap.

And then… showtime.

THE EVENING HAD GONE off without a hitch, Daphne thought, sighing as she closed the door to the inn's dining room and leaned against it, out of sight. She untied her apron and slid it off, tucking it under her arm as she headed down the hall to the inn's kitchen. There, hovering anxiously by the stacks of empty plates and the now-cold oven, was Jax. A very nervous-looking Jax, whose cheeks were bright red from standing over a hot oven for the better part of the day, his blue-green eyes glittering like jewels in the overhead lighting.

"You did an amazing job," she said, holding his gaze only long enough to give him a thumbs up before stuffing her apron into her bag. Then she collapsed onto the nearest barstool, kicked off her shoes, and began massaging her aching feet. Only a few days had passed since she'd quit her job at Sal's Diner, and already she was growing soft, she thought, wincing as she kneaded the ball of her foot. One thing she had always known was solidified tonight, though, as she scurried back and forth down the inn's long hallway, forehead dotted with sweat, arms weighed down with heavy trays of appetizers and entrees—she didn't miss waitressing at all. But this was a favor to Jax, and she had been happy to do it.

Well, she had *agreed* to do it. She couldn't say she was ever happy to be in his presence these days; more like suffocated. But that wasn't his fault, and the last thing she would ever do was let it show.

"Thank you again," Jax said, his voice a little too close for comfort—and she looked up to find him hovering over her awkwardly. He had a smear of ketchup on his stubbled chin, and she reached up without thinking to gently rub it off. She felt his breath catch when she touched him—a soft sound, barely detectable, but she recognized it all the same. After all, how many times had the same thing happened to her whenever he was near?

She immediately withdrew her hand, cheeks burning with embarrassment, and resumed massaging her feet, this time pressing into them with far more force than was necessary, a good distraction when Jax was looking at her like... that.

He opened his mouth to say something, but whatever it was, Daphne didn't want to hear it. Instead, she quickly waved her hand toward the door and said, "He's just finishing up the last few bites of his pie. He asked me to send you out so he can give his compliments to the chef. I'm sure the two of you have plenty to talk about."

Daphne had mixed feelings at those last words. She knew without a doubt that Jax had performed flawlessly tonight; my goodness, she thought, the man he was trying to impress was practically salivating every time she laid a plate in front of him, and some of the groans escaping his lips while he sucked those ribs clean were nothing short of obscene. Jax would get the job, no doubt about it. And life, for Daphne, would be much, much easier when he left.

But would it be better?

Yes, Daphne told herself firmly, her eyes on Jax's back as he tossed the dish towel slung over his shoulder onto the counter and headed for the kitchen door. Most definitely yes.

She returned her attention to her feet as he disappeared out the door, staring idly after him, her thoughts wandering, as they often did these days, to those magical summers they shared what seemed like the blink of an eye ago—her in a bikini, long legs swung over her bicycle as she pedaled beside him around town; him with his sunglasses pushed over his head, chest bare, lithe muscles on full display. So carefree, those balmy days and crisp nights stretching on endlessly, stolen kisses, hands held beneath the midnight sky, stars blanketed above them like diamonds. A perpetual summer that seemed like it would never end.

But end it did. How many summers had come and gone since then? More than she could count offhand. Still, those memories never dimmed; they burned as bright as firelight, as bright as a young girl's dreams of knights in shining armor and happily-ever-afters.

Daphne wasn't sure what carried her out of the kitchen and down the hall, stopping outside the open door to the inn's dining room, lingering just out of sight but well within earshot of the conversation. Jax had just finished greeting Steve Neuman, the man who had the last word on hiring decisions for the Miami Beach restaurant set to open in just a few months. This man, the one with the casual chinos and the turquoise polo shirt, with the tan arms and the salt-and-pepper hair, with the air of self-importance and the booming, confident voice, would be the one to decide whether Jax stayed on the island or left… this time, for good.

"It's a pleasure to meet you," Jax was saying, and Daphne scooted closer to the door, careful to keep hidden. "Thank you again for traveling all this way just to sample my food."

"The pleasure's all mine, Jax," Steve replied, scraping back his chair as, presumably, he stood to shake Jax's hand. "And I mean that wholeheartedly, especially after everything I've just tasted." He chuckled. "I've heard good things about you, which is why you've been on my radar, but this… I'll be honest with you, you just blew the competition out of the water." The sound of a hand slapping a back followed. "Right now, you're the one to beat."

What Jax said in return, Daphne would never know. She was already halfway back to the kitchen, head held high, those long-ago memories of summertimes past pushed back down below the surface.

Right where they belonged.

CHAPTER 2

Henry Turner stood in the front hallway of Edie's house, eyes locked on the front door, heart pounding in his ears. He fiddled with his watch, the soft ticking practically deafening to him as time marched steadily toward the moment when she would slot her key into the lock and turn the knob to find him standing there. Uninvited.

Was he going to give her a heart attack? The thought had occurred to him several times as he tugged uncomfortably at the collar of the dress shirt he'd bought for the occasion, the one that felt like it had been strangling him since the moment he slipped it on. He preferred soft flannel button-downs—and by soft, he meant worn down to the barest threads. Comfortable. Lived-in.

And don't even get him started about the shoes, he thought, wincing as his toes pinched together once more in the dress shoes he'd purchased and polished for the occasion. But he kept them on all the same, because he couldn't imagine what Edie would say when she realized that he was proposing to her in slippers.

It was hard to imagine now, at eighty-three years old, that he would be sharing his life with someone else. He was used to routines, to the eccentricities of his daily life: the toothpaste belonged on the second shelf in his medicine cabinet, his favorite coffee mug was hand-washed and dried every evening before bed, he always started each morning by raising the blinds three-quarters of the way up the window to provide himself with the best view of the ocean from his bedroom without being blinded by the rising sun. He liked two sugar cubes in his tea, three slices of turkey on his sandwich, and four ginger snaps as a mid-afternoon snack. Those were the things that made him *him*—idiosyncrasies that had been developed and honed over a lifetime.

A lifetime of being alone, that is.

He felt once more for the ring in his pocket, reassured when his fingers found it tucked at the very bottom, beneath his handkerchief for safekeeping.

He'd selected it just for her—an emerald surrounded by a cluster of diamonds, with a thin gold band and an inscription that he'd chosen to perfectly encapsulate what he felt for her.

Forever yours.

In truth, Edie had been his from the moment they'd met. She was new to the island then, a bubbly, vivacious woman shrouded in sorrow over the recent death of her husband, Johnny. When she walked into Henry's inn that day to ask for directions to the storefront she'd just leased, which would eventually grow into a thriving antiques shop that she still operated, she had no idea that he was the island's outcast.

By design, mostly. And years of rebuffing anyone who had shown him even an ounce of kindness.

Edie had seen through the façade, though. She'd broken down the walls, brick by brick, to reveal the man behind them. Broken and battered, but with his heart still ticking all the same.

He'd fallen for her almost immediately. It had taken him twenty years to work up the courage to ask her on a first date, and now, barely three months later, he was going to ask her to marry him. He was in love with her, and though the years in front of him numbered far fewer than the ones left behind, he couldn't imagine spending them without her by his side, every day.

He would even let her move the toothpaste. If she insisted.

Suddenly Henry straightened, hand tightening around his cane, ears perked and listening hard to the unmistakable click-click-click of Edie's heels approaching on the sidewalk. Without waiting for further confirmation, he turned and limped down the hallway toward the living room, where the dozens of rose petals awaited—in coral, her favorite color, the same shade as the sky above the island as day gave way to evening. They always sat together then, at the end of the day, hand in hand, deep in conversation until the moon dappled the water's surface, the seagulls quieted for the night, and the only thing left on the beach was the soft footprints in the sand, left behind by those who were now tucked away in their beds, shoulders freckled from another day of playing under a sun-drenched sky.

With some difficulty, Henry lowered himself to the floor in the middle of the circle of rose petals, hand braced against the nearby sofa. He heard the door creak open and then click shut, his heart in his mouth as his fingers fumbled for the ring. He retrieved it from his pocket and held it out, watching as the light from the candles he'd arranged on every surface flickered softly against the gold.

When Edie stepped into the room, unwinding the turquoise shawl she wore over her dress, she stopped dead in her tracks, her hand flying to her mouth. "Oh, my... Henry." She stood there, eyes locked with his for several long moments before she broke the connection, gazing around in disbelief at the transformation that had taken place in her living room, the one that Henry himself had painstakingly planned and carried out.

He knew this wasn't her first proposal. But he wanted it to be her last.

"Edie." His voice caught, and he cleared his throat and was about to try again when she stepped forward, shawl now abandoned on the floor, and dropped to her knees in front of him. Her eyes met his as her face softened into a smile, so beautiful and gentle and intimate—a smile meant only for him—that it nearly brought him to tears. He took a moment to compose himself, and before he tried again to speak the words that he had rehearsed so many times—long before their first date—he took her hand in his and drew it to his lips for a kiss.

"Edie," he whispered, "I love you. Would you do me the great honor of being my wife?"

The words were simple and heartfelt, like the man who spoke them.

Edie reached up to cup his face in her hands. "Oh, Henry," she said. "Believe me when I say, the honor would be mine. Of course I'll be your wife."

Her eyes were shining with tears as she stretched her hand toward him, and without a moment's hesitation, he slipped the ring on her finger, his own hands trembling as he did so. Then they kissed, her hands caressing the back of his head, him holding her as though he never wanted to let her go.

He'd waited a lifetime for this moment. And, he thought, drawing away from her with a gentle smile, he would have waited another lifetime if he had to.

Happily.

"Reed, are you *sure* you're okay?"

Tana set down her water glass for the fifth time and frowned at Reed, who was once again craning his head toward the front door. The restaurant was bustling at this hour, every corner of the entranceway crammed with patrons waiting their turn for a table, and this time, Reed actually set down his napkin and stood on tiptoe in order to see over their heads.

"If I didn't know better, I'd say he's on the lookout for his wife, terrified she's going to catch him on a date with his girlfriend," Jax teased, breaking off a piece of bread from the basket and adding a generous portion of butter. "What?" he asked as both Tana and Daphne turned to shoot him identical withering looks. "I'm only joking."

He waved the butter knife at Reed, who was still too distracted to register any portion of the conversation, let alone the fact that they were all talking about him. "Besides, he's crazy about you, Tana. Well, usually," Jax added with a grin. "Tonight, I'm not actually sure he could tell us what your name is. Want to test out the theory?" He leaned forward to tap Reed on the elbow, but Tana whacked his hand away.

"Men," Daphne muttered under her breath with a shake of her head, though Tana caught the affectionate undertone in her voice as she snuck a glance at Jax. The four of them were out to dinner to celebrate Jax's successful pitch to Steve Neuman; according to Daphne, the tasting couldn't have gone better. The restaurant investor had been gushing all the way out the inn's front door, with promises to be in touch with Jax before the end of the month. Tana was thrilled for her brother, of course, but the prospect of him moving so far away was bittersweet. She'd enjoyed their summer on the island more than she could ever say.

But that, too, was coming to an end. Over the past few days, the beaches had begun to empty out; Tana's view from the inn no longer included a sea of colorful umbrellas dotting the shoreline, and even the hot dog and ice cream vendors no longer made the trek to the sand, goodies in tow. A chill had settled over the island most mornings, requiring Tana to don a fuzzy robe and slippers before padding out to the inn's wraparound front porch to enjoy her daily routine of coffee and the sunrise. And in the evenings, long before the stars twinkled down on the half-empty boardwalk, she and Reed would wrap themselves in sweaters and blankets and sit together on the sand, watching as the mainland in the distance faded into oblivion with the setting sun.

"Where's Luke, anyway?" Jax said, nodding toward the two empty place settings at the table. Reed had mentioned that Luke and Lydia would be joining them for tonight's celebration, which Tana had found slightly odd—they'd only reconnected a few short days ago after not seeing each other for several years, and she assumed they'd want as much private time as possible right now to sort through the future of their relationship.

"Oh, I'm sure he'll be here any minute," Reed said in a vague voice, eyes still on the door as he settled back into his chair and grabbed his water glass. He gulped down half of it in one breath while Tana watched him in bemusement, noting once more his nervous fidgeting. What in the world was going on with him?

Before she could ponder the matter further, he was on his feet again, napkin fluttering to the ground as he made a beeline for the front door without bothering to excuse himself. "You're right," Daphne said, eyes on Reed's back as he wove his way through the crowd. "He is acting a bit off, isn't he?" She snuck a playful glance at Tana. "Maybe he's preparing some sort of surprise for you, like..." Her eyes lit up with excitement. "A proposal!"

"He better not be," Tana said, grabbing the butter knife from Jax and setting to work on her own slice of bread. "I'm still technically married, you know. When I get married again—*if* I get married again," she hastily corrected herself at the sight of Daphne's and Jax's raised eyebrows, "it's going to be when I'm not still legally tied to someone else. That would sort of put a damper on the whole romance of the thing, don't you think?"

As she took a bite of her bread, brushing the flaky crumbs from her mouth, her eyes sought out Reed, who was now speaking to someone by the restaurant's entrance. She couldn't see who his companion was through the ever-shifting crowd, but a stab of jealousy shot through her as he bent down to speak to the person before pulling them in for a long, tight hug. Feigning indifference, she turned back to the table only to find her brother's eyes on her and then Reed, his expression tight; Tana knew her brother was also remembering the devastation her husband Derek had wrought on her life when he had begun an affair with a woman half her age, tearing their family apart.

But Reed wasn't Derek. And Tana knew she was being ridiculous—still, those wounds were raw, and coming to a place of true healing would take time. So she supposed she was allowed to be a little ridiculous once in a while.

"Hey, it's Edie!" Daphne said as the crowd shifted once more, revealing Reed and his mother standing arm in arm. "And Henry!"

Indeed, Tana's great-uncle was standing beside them, and something about his expression was so unfamiliar, so foreign to the man she'd known since childhood, that she was immediately taken aback.

He was smiling.

And not just the tight, polite smile that he slapped on his face every now and then when manners—or Edie—dictated it; this was an ear-to-ear grin that lit up his whole face, making him look at least ten years younger. Tana craned her neck too now, and saw that he and Edie were holding hands, their fingers clasped tightly as something gold glinted on her left hand.

Heart in her throat, Tana leapt to her feet, ignoring Daphne and Jax as they called out to her. She wove through the waiters balancing trays and the diners headed to their tables, her eyes on her uncle. When she reached the small group by the front door, Reed turned toward her, his expression one of pure happiness; but for the first time since she'd met him, Tana didn't have eyes for him.

"Uncle Henry," she whispered, bypassing Reed to pull the old man in for a hug. "I'm so happy for you." She drew back to meet his gaze, holding it for several long moments, blinking back the tears that had sprung quite suddenly to her eyes. She gave his hand a gentle squeeze, a gesture that he returned before patting her softly on the cheek. Then he turned to Edie, who was watching the two of them, her fingers pressed to her lips. Tana released her uncle to embrace the older woman, who clung to her.

"Thank you," Edie said, drawing back to give Tana a tender smile. "You played no small part in bringing us together, and I want you to know that I'm forever grateful. And you." She rounded on her son, pinching his arm playfully. "How could you keep this a secret from me for so long? Haven't I raised you to tell your mother everything?"

"To be fair, it was only a few days," Reed said, chuckling as he held up his hands in surrender. "And if I'm being entirely honest, I almost accidentally spoiled the surprise on more than one occasion. That's something you haven't learned about me yet," he said, tucking his arm around Tana's waist as he led the way back to their table. "I'm a terrible secret-keeper."

"I'll keep that in mind," Tana said as she slid back into her chair and turned to Daphne and Jax, who had quickly caught on to what was happening. As they stood to congratulate the newly engaged couple, Tana smiled at Reed. "So Luke and Lydia were never planning to join us for dinner tonight, then?"

Reed snorted. "I haven't seen hide nor hair of Luke in the past three days, and I don't expect to anytime soon. Something tells me they have a lot of catching up to do." He met Tana's gaze and held it; as they stared into each other's eyes, the rest of the room fell away. "I love you," he whispered, holding out his hand, palm up, for Tana to take. She slid her fingers into his, reveling in the feeling of safety, of comfort, that always came from being in close proximity to him.

"I love you too," she mouthed back.

"Hey now, who's this celebration for, anyway?" Jax said, nudging Tana in the side and tearing her gaze away from Reed. "And speaking of which." He looked past her, raising his eyebrows in Reed's direction. "Here I was, thinking we were celebrating me and all of my amazing accomplishments. But that was all a ruse, wasn't it?"

"Guilty as charged." Reed raised his water glass in a silent toast to Jax. "But for the record, we are celebrating you, too. And Daphne, for her upcoming big day." He angled his glass toward Daphne, who gave him a shy smile. "I guess we're all filled with accomplishments these days, aren't we?" He laughed. "But yes, I couldn't tell Tana we were going out to dinner with my mother and Henry without clueing her in on what was happening. The last time Henry went on a double date was, well..." He scrunched his nose in mock-thought as Edie joined the conversation, eyes twinkling.

"Never. But I'm determined to teach this old dog a new trick or two." She glanced at Henry with an affectionate shake of her head. "I guess I've found my new mission in life."

"So Edie, tell us everything about the engagement. Were you surprised? What did he say? I need details." Daphne leaned forward eagerly, her long blonde hair falling over her shoulders.

Tana noticed her brother's gaze on Daphne's face, filled with tenderness and a longing that caused her no small amount of sadness. She knew their past was long and complicated, but those two belonged together—Tana was sure of it. She was also keenly aware that the opportunity for them to acknowledge what everyone else already knew would soon slip away, quite possibly forever. But anytime she'd attempted to broach the subject with either her brother or her best friend, she was rebuffed; eventually, she'd stopped trying altogether.

Shaking her head—and catching Reed's eye and knowing he was thinking the same thing—Tana returned her attention to the conversation. "And there he was, right on his knee in the middle of a circle of rose petals," Edie was saying, her hand resting on Henry's as she entertained the table with details of the engagement. "How he got that way in the first place, I have no idea; I practically had to call the fire department to hoist him back to his feet."

The group exploded with laughter, and even Henry joined in, his faded green eyes coming alive in a way that Tana had never seen before. She watched the couple silently for a few moments as the conversation continued around her, her heart filled with happiness that the two of them had finally found each other, but sadness, also, for the years they had let slip away by not acknowledging their true feelings sooner. She glanced at Reed then, studying the side of his face, imagining what life might look like for the two of them if they decided to grow old together.

A few months ago, the thought of being with someone other than Derek had been unimaginable. How quickly life could change.

Reed turned unexpectedly, his eyes meeting hers. He caught the wistfulness in her gaze and cocked his head slightly, a question on his face. She shook her head silently, then leaned forward to press a soft kiss to his lips. When they broke apart, her hand remained on his face, cupping his cheek, while his pale blue eyes roamed over her face.

"So have you given any thought to when the big day's going to be?" Daphne asked after giving the waiter her order and sliding her menu closed. "Next spring, maybe, or early summer, before the crowds return to the island?"

"Oh no." Edie shook her head earnestly. "Henry and I have no intentions of waiting that long—if there's one thing we've learned at our age, it's that you have to make the most of the time you have while you still can. No, we're thinking end of September." She smiled at the waiter and placed her order while a shocked silence fell over the group.

"End of September?" Tana said, leaning forward to address Edie, certain she had misheard. "But that's only a few weeks away."

"That's right." Edie and Henry shared a smile. "It's my favorite time of year, right as the seasons are changing. The island will be stunning, and we'll still be able to have an outdoor wedding." She looked around at the assembled group. "We'll just have a simple ceremony and a dinner, right on the sand. Nothing fancy, just a single evening to celebrate our love." She reached out and stroked a few wisps of

Henry's white hair, and Tana felt her eyes tearing up again.

"Well then," she announced, gripping Reed's hand, "I don't know about you, but I think we'd better skip dessert tonight. We don't have a second to waste."

CHAPTER 3

"Mom, you look... frantic."

Emery stepped up to the window beside Tana, whose nose was practically pressed against the glass as she craned to see past the inn's parking lot to the street beyond. "I absolutely am frantic," Tana said, shielding her eyes against the glaring sun as she strained to hear the sound of a distant golf cart. "And I have every right to be. This —today—is the culmination of months of hard work and stress, not to mention far more money than I care to think about."

She pressed a hand to her stomach. "I think I feel sick. What if they hate it? What if they turn right back around and leave? What if they write another awful review and post it to one of those travel websites? Or a blog? We'll be done for before we even get off the ground."

"Mom, stop." Emery tugged Tana away from the window and led her over to the inn's front desk, where a plate of food and a glass of lemonade waited. "Here. You haven't even eaten anything today, you've been so worked up. Take this." Emery passed the plate to her mother, and Tana immediately took a bite of the turkey sandwich, and then another.

"Thanks," she said, washing it down with half the glass of lemonade; she didn't realize how famished she'd been. "I told myself that I would stay busy—goodness knows there's plenty to do around here, between taking care of the inn and thinking about Uncle Henry and Edie's wedding preparations. But instead, I've been standing at this window for..." She glanced at the clock, her eyebrows shooting into her hairline. "Two hours? I don't even know what I've been doing this whole time."

"Pacing, mostly," Emery said with a smile, helping herself to a potato chip from Tana's plate. "And muttering to yourself. You look certifiable."

Tana shook her head. Count on a twenty-one-year-old to tell it like it really was. Emery had always been honest almost to the point of brutality; as a toddler, she used to go around waving a box of mints in the air, telling anyone within smelling distance that their breath was worse than the dog's. She grinned at the memory, causing her daughter to shoot her another look of concern.

"Mom, seriously, do you need me to take over? I can do the whole thing, you know—" She waved her hand vaguely in the direction of the inn's guest rooms. "Give them the key, let them know when dinner will be served."

"First of all, we don't serve dinner," Tana said with a laugh, setting down her sandwich and guiding her daughter away from the front desk. "And second of all, I'm more than capable of handling this—I'm just nervous, that's all. Now go." She shooed her daughter toward the door, where a beautiful late-summer afternoon awaited. "Enjoy the beach while you still can."

Emery grabbed a handful of chips from the plate, then allowed herself to be steered outside, almost bumping into Jax, who was making his way up the porch steps, arms loaded with groceries. "You ready for the big arrival?" he asked, holding out a bag for Tana to take. She obliged, peering inside to find eggs, oranges, pure maple syrup, and several other ingredients Jax would need to make a delicious breakfast for the guests.

"I'm counting down the minutes," Tana said, glancing once more at the clock, as though expecting time to have sped up. "I don't know why I'm so nervous," she admitted, leading Jax into the kitchen and setting the bag on the counter. They began unloading the groceries side by side. "It's the first test of what we've done here, you know? No one has stayed at the inn since the renovation, and if they don't like it… I guess it would feel like my fault, like I've somehow let Uncle Henry down." She sighed. "He couldn't even bring himself to be here. He says he and Edie are doing some things for the wedding, but I know better—he's nervous."

"It's a big deal for both of you." Jax set the bag of oranges on the countertop, and Tana eyed them, almost able to taste the freshly squeezed juice he would prepare in the morning. Then her brother turned to her, placing a hand on her shoulder. "I believe in you, and I believe in Uncle Henry. The two of you set out to reinvent this inn, and you've done it. The place looks amazing, and it's time for the rest of the world to see it too. And you know what?"

He resumed unpacking the groceries, leaning past her to slide several packages of eggs into the refrigerator. "These may be the inn's first guests, but they won't be the last. If they don't like it, what's the worst that's going to happen? They'll leave, maybe tell a few people not to come. This building"—he knocked on the kitchen's wall—"has been around for more than a hundred years. It's going to take a lot more than that to knock her down."

"You're right." Tana took a deep breath as she, too, traced her fingers along the newly painted wall. She had done right by the inn—and by Uncle Henry—and she could sleep soundly with that knowledge. But as much as she told herself that... she desperately wanted the inn to succeed. The Inn at Dolphin Bay was her first job in more than two decades outside of being a wife and mother; to Tana, it represented the chance to prove herself, to prove her worth, when she'd spent so long questioning it.

Leaving Jax to the rest of the unpacking, Tana wandered back down the inn's hallway, stopping short when she heard the unmistakable crunch of tires on gravel. She hurried to the window, peeking out from behind the curtain to see a middle-aged couple unloading a suitcase from the back of their rented golf cart. They turned, shielding their eyes from the brilliant sun as they gazed up at the inn's exterior, and the woman pointed to something on the porch before the man nodded and they headed for the steps.

Tana backed away from the curtains and hurried to the front desk, settling herself behind the computer and trying to look casual. Footsteps preceded a light knock on the door, and when she rose to open it, the couple greeted her with warm smiles. As they stepped inside, the woman looked around, her mouth slightly open as she shook her head in wonder.

"I can't believe this is the same place," she said to Tana. She ran her hands along the newly painted walls. "It's absolutely beautiful. The last time we came here, I said to Richard"—she pointed to her husband—"that I didn't know if we would ever be back. And that was such a shame, too. I can't tell you how many wonderful memories we've made here over the years. When our kids were young, we used to bring them for a week every summer."

Then she frowned at Tana, as if only truly noticing her for the first time. "The gentleman who used to run the inn. Is he…?"

The implication of the unasked question was clear, and Tana was quick to shake her head. "My great-uncle is still the inn's owner and operator. He experienced some health setbacks a few months ago and had to take some time to recover, but he's on the mend. In the meantime, I'm here to help you with anything you might need. Tell me," she said, sliding the key to their room off the hook behind the desk, "what made you give us another try?"

"We heard from a friend of ours vacationing on the island a few weeks ago that the inn was undergoing some major renovations, and that piqued our interest," the man replied. "We checked out your new website and loved the pictures, so we decided on a whim to take a little vacation, get away from it all for a few days. And being here now and seeing all the updates, I'm glad we did." As his wife nodded along eagerly, Tana began to feel her nerves melt away. As far as first impressions went, she couldn't have asked for a better one.

"Well I can't tell you how happy I am that you're here." Tana led the couple up the refinished staircase onto the second floor, stopping outside the door to the largest guest room. She paused for a moment before sliding the key into the lock and turning the handle, then stepped back as the couple entered the room, keeping her gaze locked on their faces so she could watch their reaction.

The couple headed straight for the large picture window that overlooked the harbor and, beyond it, the island's postcard-ready ocean views. The sea was a clear turquoise today, a reflection of the brilliant summer sky, and the golden sand looked inviting as the waves lapped gently against the shore. A cluster of sailboats bobbed on the horizon, and a group of kayakers—probably led by Reed—explored the waters near a rocky cove.

She stood behind the couple as they admired the scene, the woman slipping her hand into her husband's before turning to Tana. "This is absolutely lovely," she said. "The views are as incredible as I remember, and if I didn't know this was the same inn, I wouldn't have recognized it." Then she turned back to her husband. "Come on, honey, I'm dying to sink my feet into that sand."

A few minutes later, after Tana gave them a brief tour of the inn and invited them to join her for breakfast the following morning, they were out the door, striped beach towels slung over their arms, noses smeared with sunscreen. She breathed a sigh of relief when the door swung shut behind them and collapsed into the desk chair, head thrown back, eyes closed, relief washing over her in waves. She remained like that for several long moments, only opening her eyes at the sound of footsteps approaching from the kitchen.

"That bad, huh?" Jax said, taking in her slumped posture with raised eyebrows. "Don't tell me I've been slaving away in that kitchen putting away all those groceries for the past fifteen minutes with no guests to show for it." He leaned against the front desk and peered down at Tana, a smile playing across his lips. "Let me guess: they liked it."

"They *loved* it." Tana held up her hand for a high-five, which her brother returned enthusiastically. Then he tugged her up from the chair, pulling her into a bear hug that lifted her feet off the ground.

When he set her down again, his eyes were shining with happiness. "You did it, sis. You really did it."

"*We* did it," Tana said emphatically. "It's truly taken a village, and I couldn't have done it without any of you. And Luke, of course. We couldn't have picked a better contractor. He went above and beyond my wildest expectations." Spotting her cell phone beside the computer, she grabbed it and began scrolling through her contacts. "In fact, I think I'll give him a call right now. If anyone deserves a proper thank you for how the inn turned out, it's most definitely him."

"Do you really have to go?" Luke sat on the edge of the bed in Lydia's hotel room, watching her neatly fold a pair of jeans and carefully arrange them inside her suitcase. His cell phone chose that moment to begin buzzing insistently in his pocket, but he ignored it, hitting the button to silence it before returning his attention to Lydia.

"You know I do," she said, bending down to snag a pair of sandals that had worked their way under the bed. She slipped those inside the suitcase too, then padded over to the nightstand to retrieve her reading glasses and an assortment of creams and lotions whose purpose Luke couldn't even begin to deduce. He assumed, like many women who had reached their forties, she was trying to keep the wrinkles at bay, to hold onto the fountain of youth for as long as possible.

But she was as beautiful to him now as she was then; more, maybe. A lifetime had passed since they were young and in love, with stolen kisses behind the bleachers after the football games and holding each other close at the Homecoming dance morphing into something deeper, more timeless, a commitment to each other that nothing could break.

"I missed you," he said, repeating the words he'd whispered to her at least a dozen times since that moment on the beach, when they'd found each other again, their kiss amid the sand and sea solidifying what Luke had always known to be true: that they belonged together. He reached out and gently took hold of her hand; when she stopped packing and turned to him, he tugged her onto the bed beside him and wrapped his arms around her, breathing in the scent of her skin, so familiar to him, so beloved. "Please don't go."

She cupped her hands around his face, drawing him in for a kiss. When she released him, she smiled and said, "I can't just walk away from my apartment, my job. I have things to do on the mainland, but I'll be back. I promise I'll be back." She opened her mouth to say more, then hesitated and rose to her feet to resume packing instead.

Luke caught the flash of uncertainty in her eyes, and his stomach plummeted. Was she having second thoughts?

"What?" he asked, standing and turning her to face him once more. "What aren't you telling me." The ball of anxiety forming in his throat solidified as a horrible thought occurred to him. "There isn't someone else, is there?"

Lydia laughed softly as she shook her head. "There's never been anyone else, Luke. It's just..."

She hesitated again, then sighed. "You, me, this..." She waved her arm back and forth between the two of them. "I'm concerned we're jumping back into things too quickly."

"So?" Luke could hear the defensiveness in his voice. "We're not strangers off the street, Lydia. We were together for almost twenty years."

"And then apart for five." She gave him a wistful smile. "Those years apart... they changed us forever, whether we like it or not. In here." She pointed to her heart, then rested her hand on his chest, above his own heart. "I want this to work, but I want to get it right this time around—I *need* to get it right this time around. We only have one chance at this life, and I don't want to waste any more of it."

"So what are you saying?" By now, Luke was thoroughly confused; it sounded like she was talking in circles, and his instincts were warning him that this conversation was entering dangerous territory. The past few days together had been nothing short of pure bliss, and naïve or not, he wanted to keep it that way.

Lydia, it seemed, had other plans.

"Stop looking so concerned," she said, batting him on the chest before stepping back from him and taking both of his hands in her own. "All I'm saying is that I want to start fresh, with a solid foundation and a clean slate, for both of us." She met his eyes. "In order to do that, I'd like for you to agree to two things."

"Anything," he responded without hesitation. Could he say anything else when she was looking at him like that? He would lasso every star in the sky for her, if he could—whatever it took to keep them together. He lost her once, and it almost destroyed him; this time, he couldn't risk that happening again.

She took a deep breath. "Number one, I don't want us to rush into anything we aren't ready for. Like getting remarried, or moving in together, or anything serious like that."

"Okay..." Luke said slowly, considering her words. Then he nodded, albeit reluctantly. "I can do that." He scratched his hand idly down his stubbled cheeks. "So, what, you want to... date again?"

"I do." Lydia nodded, then crossed her arms over her chest, her posture almost defensive. "Will that be too weird for you?"

"On the contrary," Luke said, a slow smile spreading across his face as he reached for her and tugged her onto his lap, "I think it's an incredible idea."

"You do?" Doubt flickered in her eyes as she

wound her arms around his neck. "I thought you'd think it was ridiculous. I mean, we dated for how many years before we got married. Six? Seven?" She laughed. "I don't even know how to date anymore."

"You just leave that part to me." Luke tightened his arms around her and gazed up into her face before brushing back a strand of hair that had fallen over her cheek. "I would love to have a chance to woo you all over again. I'm an expert wooer, you know." He gave her a mischievous grin. "As I'm sure you remember."

"I remember you forgetting your wallet for our first official date and me having to pick up the tab at the restaurant." Lydia smirked at the memory. "Is that what expert wooers usually do?"

"If it gives them a chance to stop over at your house later that night to pay you back, it most certainly is." Then he gave her a playful shove, sliding her off his lap. "Excuse me, miss, we hardly know each other. Why don't you at least let me take you out to dinner first? I'm an honorable man, you know."

She laughed, and he could see her tension melting away as she stepped over to the suitcase to resume packing. "Thank you," she said quietly a few moments later, holding a pair of socks as she met

Luke's eyes. "I appreciate that you're willing to do this, and keep a sense of humor about it too. And also"—she took a deep breath and let it out slowly, her gaze straying to the floor—"I want to thank you." She swallowed hard. "It's no secret that I broke your heart when I walked out the door. I wasn't in my right head, but that doesn't excuse what I did, how I gave up on us when you begged me not to. It takes a special person to not hold that against me."

Luke was silent for several long moments after that as he digested her words, the memories of the last days of their marriage playing through his mind. "I never blamed you," he said softly. "Not entirely. We both played a part in what happened, but at the same time, neither one of us were at fault. The things that happened to us, the loss we experienced..."

His voice caught as he was immediately thrust back into those dark days, those dark *years*, of trying to start a family. Then he looked up and met her gaze, holding it steadily.

"Most people would have broken long before us. It's a testament to what we mean to each other that we were able to lean on each other for as long as we did." He stood and spun her toward him, then wrapped his arms around her waist and held her close. "As far as I'm concerned, there's nothing to forgive. Like you said, I want to move forward, do our best to start fresh and put the past behind us."

Then he pulled away from her with a slight frown. "You said there were two things you wanted us to do. What's the second?"

"I'd like for us to see a marriage counselor, at least a couple of times, to help us work through some of our issues and rebuild the foundation of our relationship. A few of my girlfriends have gone to therapy with their husbands, and they've all said it's done wonderful things for them. I think, given everything we've gone through, it would help for us to have some outside guidance while we figure out our future."

She seemed to be holding her breath once more, as though expecting him to argue—and while Luke had to privately admit that he wasn't crazy about the idea of baring his soul to a complete stranger, he would go to the ends of the earth if it meant he could call Lydia his again.

And so, pushing aside any reservations he might have, he kissed her softly on the lips and said, "I think that's a great idea. Sign me up."

CHAPTER 4

"Here I am, at your service." Jax tipped his baseball cap jauntily as he stood in the doorway to Daphne's apartment, arms weighed down with baking supplies.

"Thank you, thank you, *thank* you." Daphne swung the door open wide and practically yanked him inside. The bakery was set to open in less than twenty-four hours, and to say she was frantic would be the understatement of the century. She'd been up since before the sunrise, rolling and mixing and kneading and icing, every surface of her kitchen coated in flour, sugar, and tepid mugs of half-drunk coffee that she'd been consuming round the clock to keep herself focused... and semi-awake.

"Whoa." Jax stopped short in the kitchen doorway, taking in the chaos with a bemused expression. "It looks like a bomb went off in here." He nudged aside a pile of unwashed mixing bowls stacked on the counter to set down the supplies she'd asked him to grab for her last-minute. "Here are your chocolate chips." He grinned at her as he held them up. "You know, for the chocolate chip cookies you're supposed to be making?" He eyed the trash can, which was overflowing with several dozen discarded chocolate chip cookies—sans chocolate chips, which a distracted Daphne had forgotten to add.

And then promptly beat herself up over for the next hour, tears of stress and anxiety streaming down her face. If she couldn't even get a basic batch of cookies right, how in the world was she going to successfully run an entire bakery?

"This was a mistake," Daphne moaned as she grabbed the chocolate chips from Jax and began rooting around in her cabinets for a clean mixing bowl, to no avail. "I'm a complete disaster, and it's not even day one. What was I thinking, trying to do this all on my own? I have no idea how to run a business. This was a crazy idea, and now I'm in over my head." She squirted dish soap onto a rag and began frantically scrubbing out one of the bowls until Jax took it from her, nudging her aside so he could take her place.

"You know how to bake—your desserts are some of the best I've ever tasted." When Daphne opened her mouth to protest, Jax held up a soapy hand to stop her. "Take that with a grain of salt if you want to, but let me remind you that I've worked behind the scenes at plenty of popular restaurants in my day, and each one of them had their own pastry chef. And not one of them could hold a candle to you."

He finished scrubbing out the bowl, then rinsed it out, raising his voice so Daphne could hear him over the water. "The business side of things is daunting—believe me, I get it. But the more experienced you get at that side of it, the more confident you'll become, and eventually it'll be second nature. Besides," he said, adding more soap to the dish pan and grabbing several more bowls, "it's not like you'll be alone. You have Tana, and Luke. And me. I don't know if you know this about me, but I understand a thing or two about running a business." Then he winced. "As long as one of your trusted employees isn't stealing money from you and bleeding you dry, you'll be golden."

Daphne gave him a sympathetic look; she knew Jax hadn't fully recovered—would perhaps never fully recover—from that betrayal. And if he could pick up the pieces of his life after losing everything he had, and meet new opportunities that came his way with open arms, then maybe she needed to look to him as an example, and stop obsessing so much about every little thing that could go wrong.

And speaking of new opportunities...

She felt her heart sinking as she snuck a glance at Jax, who was now standing beside a pile of clean dishes, whistling as he worked. Had he heard back from the restaurant investor yet? She couldn't bring herself to ask, because she was afraid to hear the answer. Not that it would be a surprise—Jax had that job in the bag, and his time on the island was limited. When she reminded him of that now, he merely gave a nonchalant shrug, his eyes still on the dishes.

"That's why they invented telephones. You can call me up anytime you have a question—I'll drop everything I'm doing to answer it." He looked up, meeting her gaze, his eyes filled with sincerity. "And that's a promise."

Daphne laughed, though the sound came out slightly strangled. "You say that now, but when you're a bigshot Miami chef, you're not going to have time for little old me. Don't worry, I'll understand. Maybe just shoot me a postcard once in a while, let me know you're still alive."

Jax snorted and shook his head. His hands stilled on the dishes for a moment, fingers dripping with suds, and then he turned to her, giving her his full attention. "Daphne, I will *always* have time for you. When are you going to realize that you're the one holding all the cards here?" A look of sadness, of frustration, crossed his face, and when he returned to the dishes, Daphne could see that he was scrubbing them harder than he had been a moment ago.

She watched him, her eyes on the side of his face, noting the tension in his jaw. Then her gaze wandered to the hollow of his neck, her fingers flexing automatically as she remembered how many times they'd caressed the soft skin there, one of many favorite spots on his body she'd explored all those years ago. Heart in her throat, she took a step forward, and then another; hearing her approach, Jax swung his head toward her, and their eyes met—his wistful, hers laced with confusion.

A sudden pounding interrupted the moment, and Daphne jumped back, heart jackhammering, as she looked around wildly for the source of the sound. "Someone's at the door," Jax said, tilting his head toward the living room, his voice tight with annoyance.

"Oh, right." Daphne swung around, glad for the interruption, her pulse still racing. She didn't give Jax a backward glance as she hurried to the door, yanking it open without bothering to look through the peephole—right now, whoever was on the other side was more than welcome to come in, up to and including door-to-door salesmen, political canvassers, and kidnappers.

"Edie!" she said when she saw the older woman standing outside her apartment. "What a lovely surprise! What can I do for you today?" Daphne's voice sounded manic, even to her own ears, but if Reed's mother noticed, she had far too much grace to point it out.

She also didn't miss a beat, though, stepping into the apartment and immediately tipping her head toward the kitchen, where Jax was still clattering away at the dishes, though he was no longer whistling. "Am I interrupting something? Tana mentioned that her brother was stopping by today to help you with a few… things." The suggestion in her tone was unmistakable, and Daphne immediately felt her cheeks coloring with embarrassment.

"Yes, I gave him a hand during his interview last week with that restaurant investor, and he's returning the favor by helping me prepare for the bakery's opening."

"Ah, yes, tomorrow's the big day." Edie settled herself onto Daphne's couch and arranged her dress neatly around her knees. "Some of my friends and I will be there bright and early, of course. We can't wait to support you. I plan on saving my appetite today so I can indulge tomorrow—I hear you make a cherry strudel that's out of this world. I've also been spreading the word to everyone who comes into my shop, and they've promised to make an appearance."

"Thank you," Daphne said, feeling her eyes well up with tears and then immediately chastising herself internally for the unnecessary display of emotion. She was letting her anxiety get the better of her—why else would she be in such a state? And why else would she have almost, *almost,* let herself slip with Jax?

It was nerves. It had to be. There was no other explanation.

"It's my pleasure, my dear," Edie said with a soft

smile. "We islanders always take care of our own, and you're a beloved member of this community."

"Edie! Tired of my uncle already?"

Daphne swung around to find Jax in the kitchen doorway, wiping his hands on a dish towel. He studiously avoided Daphne's gaze as he strode forward to greet Edie with a kiss on the cheek. "How's the wedding planning going? It's practically all Tana can talk about—she hasn't been this excited about something in, well... ever." He grinned at her. "I'm pretty sure she's living vicariously through you right now—she's got wedding fever. And don't tell Reed I said that. Don't want to scare the poor guy off."

"Oh, I don't think there's any danger of that," Edie said, eyes twinkling playfully. "But to answer your question, the wedding planning is off to a good start—my daughters and I already have an appointment at a bridal salon on the mainland to try on dresses. And that leads me to the next item on my list."

She turned to Daphne. "I know you have a lot going on right now, and the last thing I want to do is be a bother... so please, feel free to say no. You won't hurt my feelings, Scout's honor." She held up her hand. "But Tana mentioned a few weeks ago that you were interested in designing cakes, and it's stuck in my mind since then, so I was wondering... would you be willing to bake our wedding cake? Nothing fancy," she added hastily. "Just a simple design, basic flavors. God forbid Henry steps outside the vanilla box." She shook her head affectionately. "It's taken all my strength trying to convince him to wear a proper suit for the wedding. If that old kook had his way, he'd be walking down the aisle in those ratty old slippers of his."

As Jax chuckled appreciatively, Edie smiled at Daphne. "Let me reiterate that you won't hurt my feelings if you don't have the time or the inclination. But I don't know a more talented baker around than you, so I had to ask."

She and Jax both watched Daphne, waiting for her response, and she could feel her eyes clouding with tears once more. "I would be honored," she said, pressing a hand to her chest before bending down to hug the older woman. Edie was the most generous person Daphne knew, and a kind, gentle soul who had become an integral member of the Dolphin Bay community since she'd moved here twenty years ago. If anyone deserved the wedding—and the cake—of their dreams, it was her.

Daphne released Edie from the hug and rose to

her feet once more. "I've been trying to figure out the perfect gift for you and Mr. Turner, and now I have it—the cake. Please accept it as my wedding present to you, with my best wishes for a long and happy life together."

She could feel Jax's eyes on her as she spoke, but she wouldn't—couldn't—bring herself to meet his gaze. Instead, she kept her focus on Edie, watching as the bride-to-be's face lit up with happiness.

"You're too kind. I would normally say I couldn't accept such a generous gift, but to heck with it, I *am* the bride. I might as well enjoy some of the perks that come along with it, right?" She grinned at Daphne, who laughed as she bent down once more to hug Edie.

"Congratulations again," she whispered into the older woman's soft white hair. "I couldn't be happier for you and Henry. Truly."

"Thank you." Edie patted her on the shoulder. "And I couldn't be happier for you either, my dear girl."

Daphne shook her head ruefully as she pulled away from Edie. "Let me get through my first day without anything awful happening, and *then* you can be happy for me."

Edie laughed softly and shook her head. "Oh,

honey, I didn't mean the bakery." Her eyes flicked to Jax, who was heading back to the kitchen, whistling once more. Then she winked at Daphne before giving her another pat on the shoulder and heading for the door.

CHAPTER 5

"Well, Henry, I have to say, I'm impressed." Ian Cooper, Henry's physical therapist, shook his head in amazement as Tana's uncle navigated the room without his cane for the first time since the stroke that had left him hospitalized. Since Henry had been released, Tana had accompanied him to therapy twice a week religiously, and oversaw his exercises at home to ensure he had the best chances of regaining use of his left side, which had been left partially immobilized. When he started physical therapy at the beginning of summer, Tana feared her uncle would never walk independently again; now, he was thriving.

And she knew the newfound love in his life had played no small roll in his recovery. Henry Turner had a lot to live for these days; the gruff, standoffish man Tana had seen in that hospital bed—and indeed, for all of her childhood—had been replaced by a softer man, one who was quicker with a smile or a laugh, one who was no longer afraid to wear his heart on his sleeve.

He had grown. So, too, had Tana.

As much as she wanted her uncle to recover, and to live a full, healthy life, part of her couldn't help the sadness she felt as she watched her uncle's cane lying abandoned on the floor. When she had first arrived in Dolphin Bay, suitcase in hand, heartbroken and scared, her duties were simple: help Uncle Henry with the inn, since he wasn't healthy enough to manage it on his own. Even though she'd had no experience running an inn, or doing much else outside of being a wife and mother, Tana had stepped up to the challenge as best as she could. Since then, the inn had become her passion, her solace, her shelter from a world that could sometimes be harsh and unforgiving.

She loved the inn. And she loved her role within it.

But now, she couldn't ignore the truth creeping up on her: soon, she would no longer be needed. The inn belonged to Uncle Henry; the inn *was* Uncle

Henry. She would have no place there anymore, outside of being an occasional visitor.

What then?

"I told you I was going to dance at my wedding," Henry said, limping slightly as he turned and made his way back to Ian, who was looking on with pride. "I made a promise to Edie, and I intend on keeping it." His eyes met Tana's, and she could see that his face was practically glowing. She swallowed the lump in her throat and grinned at him.

Where was she going to find a job? And moreover, who was going to hire her? Dolphin Bay was a tiny island, with most of its residents either owning businesses of their own—like Henry, Reed, Edie, and, soon, Daphne—or working on the mainland. The thought of going on interviews sent a shiver of fear running through Tana; what would she even put on her resume? Job experience: None. Unless you counted raising an amazing daughter, of course, which was and always would be the most important job of Tana's life. Somehow, though, she didn't think a potential employer would see it that way.

And even more important than that, Tana had no idea what she wanted to do with the rest of her life. The only thing that came to mind was operating a small inn or bed and breakfast of her own, but that was off the table entirely—no way was she going to create any kind of competition for her uncle, especially after all that he'd been through over the past few years.

So it was with a sinking feeling in her stomach that Tana boarded the ferry a short while later with her uncle, helping him navigate the ramp and settle into his seat, even though she could tell he was perfectly capable of doing it on his own. After greeting Kurt, the friendly captain, and smiling at her fellow passengers, most of whom were residents of the island returning from a morning of shopping or appointments on the mainland, she sank into the seat beside Henry, hands clutched around her purse.

A few minutes later, the ferry was gliding out of the harbor, and Tana pulled her sweater tighter around her shoulders as the wind kicked up, sending a fine spray of sea mist over her face and hands. Abandoning the usual conversation she tried to engage her uncle in during these ferry rides, Tana opted for silence instead, but she knew the serene expression on her face as she enjoyed the sun's rays belied the turmoil beneath the surface. She had known her time at the inn would someday come to an end, of course. She just didn't realize it would be so soon.

"What's going on in that head of yours, kid?"

Tana turned to find her uncle watching her curiously, his hands settled in his lap, cane once more lying on the floor. When he saw her gaze straying to it, he said, "Ah," with a single knowing nod. Arranging himself in his chair so that they were facing each other—another oddity for Henry Turner, a man who had always preferred as little eye contact as possible—he patted her knee and said, "You know you'll always have a place at the inn."

"I know." Tana averted her eyes from his face, turning instead to the horizon. In the distance, the island was just coming into view, a hazy purple outline against a backdrop of blue sky and crystalline water. Somewhere on that island were nearly all of the people she loved, and that knowledge brought her a sense of peace despite the uncertainty surrounding her.

Then she turned back to her uncle and smiled. "But the inn is yours, and it always will be. I've gone through a lot these past few months, trying to find my place in this world, and it seems I'm not quite finished yet. I still have a lot of decisions to make. And that's not a bad thing, it's just..."

She let her voice trail off as she thought back to her former life in California—the wealthy friends, the enviable zip code, the industry parties where she always felt like an outsider. She hadn't found her place in that world, either.

Where *did* she belong?

"You'd like to be settled." Uncle Henry finished the sentence for her, and Tana was surprised at how accurately he had captured what she was feeling. Perhaps there had always been far more going on beneath the surface of this man than anyone had suspected.

"Yes," she acknowledged. "I want to feel… safe, I guess. Happy. And I do—most of the pieces are in place. But I guess after so many months of uncertainty, I'd like to have my future mapped out for me." She laughed. "Which is ridiculous; I know that. No one has any idea what the future holds."

"You can only make the choices that feel right for you, that feel right in here." Uncle Henry thumped his chest, then his gaze traveled past her to the water beyond. "The rest of life… well, we all just stumble through it the best we can, don't we? And hope, in the end, that it all works out."

Tana knew he was thinking about Penny, the girl he once loved. He had chosen a life on the island over her, and even though the decision had haunted him for years, he hadn't been able to bear the idea of leaving the home he loved so dearly. But now, he had Edie—his happy ending.

"I guess I just have to be patient," she said with a sigh. "And trust that things will work out."

"That's all we can do," Henry murmured, so softly Tana could barely hear him over the wind and the waves. "That's all anyone can do."

They both watched the water for a time after that, each lost in thought. What seemed like moments later, Tana felt a jolt as the ferry glided to a stop in the Dolphin Bay harbor, and looked up to find that her fellow passengers were already gathering their things and heading for the ramp, preparing to disembark.

She and Henry followed suit, although at a slower pace, waving goodbye to Kurt and making their way along the wide dirt path that led to the edge of town. The trip took longer than usual because her uncle insisted on forgoing his cane, but Tana didn't mind—it was a beautiful day, one of the last golden summer afternoons they would experience on the island for quite some time. She felt slightly melancholy about the changing seasons, but at least they all had the wedding to look forward to, a celebration of love that would carry them through the winter months.

Henry, too, must have been thinking about his upcoming wedding, for as they rounded the final bend in the path, dune grass brushing against their ankles, he glanced at Tana and said, "Do you think your mother will come?"

Tana was taken aback by the unexpected question. She hadn't even considered that Julie Keller would attend Henry and Edie's wedding. Their mother had largely been absent from Tana and Jax's childhood, which was why they had spent their summers with Uncle Henry at the inn. Her job as a wildlife photographer carried her to far-flung places of the globe, but even in the rare times when she was present in her children's lives, she was never really… present.

In the years since, Tana had cobbled together somewhat of a relationship with her, keeping things cordial but distant. Jax had a much more difficult time reconciling the mother they had with the one they deserved, and wouldn't take her presence on the island lightly.

"To be honest, Uncle Henry, I didn't even think to call her."

Was that a flash of disappointment on her uncle's face? Tana immediately felt annoyed at herself for the oversight.

"How about I give her a call tonight?" she added hastily. "It's been a while since we've caught up anyway. But—" She hesitated, unsure how best to proceed. "Julie's always been a little… flighty. I'm not sure we can count on her as one of the guests."

Even if she said she would be there, Tana thought privately, but didn't want to hurt her uncle's feelings by voicing that uncomfortable truth out loud. If Tana knew one thing about her mother, it was that Julie Keller wasn't someone you could rely on. Unless you were a lion on the African savanna with dreams of being on the cover of *National Geographic*, that is. No one else—child or otherwise—seemed to matter much.

Henry fell silent for a few minutes after that, the only sound his steady breathing as he navigated the dirt path with some difficulty. Tana debated reaching out a hand to help him on more than one occasion, but always ended up stopping herself; she could tell by her uncle's expression of steely-eyed resolve that this was something he needed to do alone, a challenge where he was determined to be the victor.

When they finally reached the end of the path and the inn's roof came into view, Henry stopped to take a break, breathing heavily while Tana looked on in concern. Then he limped forward with renewed determination, her by his side, their feet crunching on the inn's gravel driveway.

As they crossed the driveway, Tana couldn't help the feeling of pride that surged within her as she counted the rental golf carts parked there: three in total, each belonging to a couple who were staying at the inn. The reservations had been trickling in steadily over the past week, helped along by the recent publicity the inn's renovations had received, and with each key she passed into a guest's waiting hand, Tana's confidence blossomed to new heights.

Her mind elsewhere, Tana didn't realize her uncle had stopped walking until she almost collided with him at the bottom of the inn's porch steps. He was staring up at the front door, his gaze oddly vacant, and when Tana rested a hand on his shoulder, he startled a bit before turning to her.

"You know, I never had children of my own," he said, his voice soft, a hint of sadness echoing through it. "Your mother—we used to be close. She's the nearest thing I have to a daughter of my own." He took a deep breath, almost as if stealing himself for the words to come.

"I'm a simple man, and I don't have a lot of requests." By now, he was practically whispering, and Tana had to lean in closer to hear him. "But I would really love it if she would come."

Reaching forward to give the old man's hand a gentle squeeze, Tana said, "I'm sure she wouldn't want to miss it. I'll see what I can do."

And even though her words left a soft smile on Uncle Henry's lips, Tana was having a hard time ignoring the pit of doubt that had opened in her own stomach, warning her of disappointments to come.

CHAPTER 6

"Okay, ready? On three, say 'cheese danish.' One, two, two and a quarter, two and a half..."

"Jax, please, just take the picture!" Daphne shifted awkwardly from foot to foot beneath the yellow and white awning as she glanced up and down the street, hoping none of the island's residents or tourists were out for an early morning stroll. She hated having her picture taken on a good day, always horrified to see the final product, where she inevitably looked like a troll who'd eaten a bad batch of snails.

But today, when her eyes were rimmed with purple from the sleepless night, her heart was racing erratically, and her clothes were already covered in powdered sugar and flour? Five more seconds of this, and she would march right over to Jax and slap that camera right out of his hand. And the smirk right off his face too, for good measure.

Click click click.

Jax snapped photo after photo as Daphne gave him a pained smile, and then finally, mercifully, he palmed his phone to swipe through his handiwork. "Well?" she asked, walking over to him and craning her neck for a better look. "How are they?"

"They're…" He paused and scratched his chin idly while searching for the right word. "You look…" He pursed his lips and squinted at her. "The word 'constipated' comes to mind."

"Always the charmer." Daphne grabbed the phone from him and slid it into her own pocket, ignoring his protests. Then she turned and gazed up at the awning, and the sign above it, its white letters highlighted against the sun-streaked golden sky.

Sugarbloom.

She'd agonized over the bakery's name for weeks, hounding her friends endlessly for suggestions, when one night, as she stared up at the ceiling, watching the shadows dance patterns above her, it popped into her head without warning and stayed there, the perfect blend of sweet and contemporary that she had always envisioned.

"Are you ready?" Jax asked, slinging an arm over her shoulders as they stood together, staring at the bakery, still and silent at this early hour. "This is the last time you're going to see it empty like this—in a few hours, it's going to be bursting with customers." He nodded at the stacks of containers at their feet, filled to the brim with the pastries that Daphne had been working round the clock to finish before the bakery's grand opening.

"I hope so," she murmured, leaning into him for the briefest of moments before catching herself and straightening, sidestepping his arm to crouch down beside the containers instead.

Jax pretended not to notice her slip away from him, but she caught the flash of hurt in his eyes all the same as she straightened up, balancing several containers of cookies in her hands, and passed them into his waiting arms.

"Remind me again why you didn't just make all this stuff in your bakery's actual, you know, *kitchen*?" he teased as they headed toward the front door, arms weighed down with pastries. "I'm going to have to confiscate at least three dozen of these snicker-doodles as payment for the pain and suffering I endured loading all of these into your golf cart this morning."

"Because," Daphne said, shifting the containers to one hand so she could use the other to dig around in her pocket for the bakery's keys, "I feel much more at ease in my own kitchen. I'm sure that will change, but right now, with everything happening so fast..." She slid the key into the bakery's front door and kneed it open gently, taking a deep breath as she looked around the dim interior. "I need something familiar in my life right now."

Was it strange that, in that moment, she desperately missed her job at Sal's? She'd waitressed at the island's popular diner for twenty-seven years, since she was nothing more than a kid, and even though she'd always dreamed of striking out on her own, now that the day had finally arrived where that had become a reality...

She was terrified. Absolutely, positively terrified.

"It's all going to work out just fine," Jax said, coming to a stop beside her. He reached out a hand to flick on the light, and the bakery's interior bloomed to life. "Right now, you need to just get through this one day. Correction: *we* need to just get through this one day."

Daphne frowned as Jax's words registered. "What

do you mean, we?" she asked, turning to him. The bakery's soft lighting highlighted the strands of silver in his dark hair, causing her breath to hitch; in what seemed like the blink of an eye, he'd transformed from the boy she'd loved in childhood to the man standing before her, weathered by life and the passage of time. He was still as handsome as ever, though, and when his striking blue-green eyes met hers, for once, she allowed herself to hold his gaze.

His expression softened as his eyes roamed over her face, just for a moment, before he turned away from her to set the containers he'd been carrying on a nearby table. "I've cleared my schedule for the whole day to help you—if you'll have me, that is."

There was longing in those last words, an unspoken implication that he meant more than just today. But then he gave her his characteristic mischievous grin and popped the top off the nearest container, helping himself to a chocolate cupcake. "Fuel for the day ahead," he said, taking an enormous bite before passing a second cupcake to Daphne. "Trust me, I have a feeling we're going to need plenty of it."

"I hope you're right," Daphne said, considering the cupcake for a moment before shrugging and taking an equally enormous bite. When all else failed, sugar was the answer; that should be her new motto, she decided.

Wiping a smear of frosting from her top lip, she stared out the window and asked softly, "What if no one comes?" It was the first time she was giving voice to the fears that had plagued her every day since she'd signed the lease and started transforming the rental space into the bakery that now stood before her.

"Oh, they'll come," Jax said, polishing off his own cupcake and then grabbing a stack of containers before heading over to the gleaming cases awaiting her creations, empty and inviting. "Everyone on this island loves a good cupcake. And more importantly," he said, offering her a smile over his shoulder, "everyone on this island loves *you*."

TANA GLANCED at the clock as she swept mascara over her lashes, ran a comb through her hair, and grabbed her purse before heading down the staircase to the inn's foyer. Her stomach was dancing with nerves, and she didn't even know why—after all, she wasn't the one launching a new bakery today. But she'd been by Daphne's side every step of the way over the past few months as she made the transition from unhappy waitress to full-fledged business owner, providing a shoulder to lean on when the fears and uncertainties came through, and a cheerleader when each new step was accomplished.

So in a way, Sugarbloom felt like her bakery too —and she intended to spend plenty of time there, today included. Fortunately, Uncle Henry had agreed to handle the inn while she was gone, and Jax had shown up at the kitchen before dawn to prepare a quick but delicious breakfast for the guests that Tana had served so he could help Daphne with the morning's preparations.

Now, there was nothing left to do but enjoy Sugarbloom's grand opening, and Tana was itching to step inside and congratulate her friend… not to mention sample a donut or two.

So when Reed strolled up the inn's cobblestone sidewalk a few minutes later to accompany her to the bakery, sunglasses pushed casually over his head, he was greeted by an impatient Tana who was tapping her foot and looking at her watch pointedly.

"What?" He frowned as he took in her expression. "Am I late?"

Tana didn't answer, instead bounding down the porch steps and tugging his arm until he was heading back in the opposite direction with her, toward the town's main square. "Nervous?" he asked, giving her an amused smile as she strode down the street, not bothering to check if he was keeping up. A seagull soared overhead, following their progress, its beady eyes searching the island's pristine sidewalks for any discarded food wrappers but coming up empty.

"And hungry." Tana grinned at him over her shoulder as they sidestepped a family of tourists heading toward the beach, umbrella and towels in tow, flip-flops smacking against the sidewalk. They were becoming fewer and farther between these days; soon, schools would be opening for the year, the vacationers would trickle back to the mainland, and the island's beautiful golden-sand beaches would be covered with the drifting leaves of autumn.

Tana felt a hand slipping into hers, warm and reassuring, and she smiled softly at Reed as he gently tugged her back toward him so that they were walking close together. "What's the hurry?" he murmured in her ear as he released her hand and slipped his arm around her waist instead, pulling her close to him. "We've got plenty of time."

With that, he squeezed her waist, then led her to an out-of-the-way pocket of the town square, where a gap in the buildings overlooked a breathtaking expanse of coastline surrounded by wild dune grass blowing softly in the wind. Her hair whipped around her face as he turned her to face him, tucking the stray strands behind her ears before tipping her chin up and kissing her, his lips leisurely exploring hers as she wound her arms around his neck. When they broke apart, his eyes lingered on hers for several long moments, and then he moved to stand behind her, arms wrapped around her waist as they watched the sailboats dotting the horizon.

Tana's heart ached with happiness as she leaned into his chest, soaking in this moment, the one that she never would have dreamed possible a few months ago, when the life she used to know lay shattered at her feet. How things had changed since then, she thought as the wind kicked up, sending a mist of saltwater over them, causing her to shiver and draw deeper into his arms. How wonderful life had become.

For a few blissful moments, she set aside her worries about her diminishing role at the inn, which was only highlighted by her uncle's eagerness to step in today in her place. She may not know exactly what the future held for her... but this man who held her tight was most definitely going to be part of it.

Reed unwound his arms from her waist and kissed her one last time before stepping back with a grin. "Okay, *now* I'm ready to go." She laughed and tucked her hand inside his, and together they strolled down the street, slower this time, enjoying the view and each other's company. When they rounded a bend in the road and Daphne's bakery came into view, Tana stopped short, tugging Reed to a halt beside her.

"Am I seeing what I think I'm seeing?" Tana's eyes were wide with disbelief as she took in the line of customers that wrapped around the corner and stretched down the street. She recognized many of them as the island's year-round residents and shop owners who had come out bright and early to support one of their own. She squinted, seeing her brother moving down the line, passing out what looked like free cookies to the waiting crowd.

Tana hurried forward, Reed at her side, and when Jax spotted her, he raised his hand in a wave before handing out the last of the cookies and jogging over to their side. His face was bright red, his forehead was beaded with sweat, and his T-shirt and jeans had several smears of frosting on them. But he looked positively elated, beaming ear to ear as he stopped in front of them.

"It's been an absolute madhouse," he said, tucking the empty tray under his arm and gesturing to the crowd. "Before we even opened the doors, there was a line of customers outside, and it's only grown longer as the morning has passed. I haven't been able to step away for a second to catch my breath." He wiped the back of his free hand across his brow and shook his head in wonder as he surveyed the crowd.

"How's Daphne?" Reed asked as Tana stood on tiptoe, picking out faces she knew from the crowd. "Is she holding up okay?"

"She's on cloud nine." Jax grinned. "When we first opened the door and everybody started piling in, I thought she was going to have a heart attack. But she caught her stride almost immediately—you should see her, Tana," he said, turning to his sister. "It's like she's been doing this her whole life." The pride in his tone was unmistakable.

"I can't tell you how happy I am to hear that," Tana said, relief for her friend washing over her. Hopefully the warm welcome the bakery was receiving would go a long way toward bolstering Daphne's self-esteem. She grabbed Reed's hand. "Come on, let's take our place at the back of the line. It'll give us a chance to work up even more of an appetite." Tana started walking away, but her brother held out a hand, barring her from moving toward the crowd.

"Oh no you don't." He gave a firm shake of his head.

"Jax, we would never even think of cutting in line ahead of all these people," Tana said, waving her arm toward the line; even as they stood there, it had grown longer by at least a few storefronts.

"Sweet of you." Jax grinned down at her. "But that's not what I meant."

He tugged her off to the side, with Reed following behind them, then led them down a small alleyway between buildings before stopping at the bakery's back entrance. He opened the door and ushered them into the kitchen, grabbing two spare white aprons hanging on a nearby hook and thrusting them out to the pair.

"Here you go. Put them on and wash your hands. Oh, and grab a drink of water and a donut, too." He jabbed his thumb over his shoulder, indicating a plate of donuts sitting on the counter. "You're going to need your strength."

Then he was gone, elbowing open the kitchen door and disappearing into the bakery's main area, where Tana could hear the crowd chattering in excitement as they perused the cases loaded with Daphne's goodies.

Tana stared down at the apron in her hands in bewilderment, then glanced at Reed, who was in the process of unfolding his own apron and tying it around his waist. He swept his gaze around the kitchen before spotting the sink and making a beeline for it, Tana on his heels.

"What just happened?" she asked, watching as he squirted soap onto his hands and lathered up.

"We've been drafted," he responded, drying his hands on a paper towel. He tossed the roll to Tana, who barely caught it before it hit the ground. Then, with a wink and a salute, he followed Jax into the bakery to greet the waiting crowd.

CHAPTER 7

Lydia was just adding the finishing touches to her makeup when she heard the knock at the door, frowning as she noted the time. Luke was early, which, frankly, was unlike him. The man had to set three alarms just to get up in the morning, and don't even get her started on how many times during their marriage they'd missed the first few minutes of a movie playing at the small theater in downtown Dolphin Bay while she waited for him to finish getting ready.

She smiled to herself as she added a dab of rose-water perfume to her neck and wrists. Maybe he was as excited—and impatient—for their date as she was.

After scrutinizing her reflection a final time, Lydia smoothed down the creases on the red dress she'd chosen for the occasion and grabbed her heels, letting them dangle from one hand as she padded barefoot down the hallway of her apartment toward the front door. Setting them on the floor, she took a deep breath, hand on the knob, and opened the door, her heart leaping into her throat.

And then plummeting right back down again.

"Mom, what are you *doing* here?" she hissed, glancing up and down the street to make sure Luke was nowhere in sight and praying that his perpetual lateness would play out in her favor this time. She stepped into the doorway, arms crossed over her chest, blocking her mother's entrance.

"What do you mean, what am I doing here?" Wilma Peterson looked wounded, her eyes large and round as she took in her daughter's annoyance. "I'm here to say hello to my only son-in-law. I haven't seen him in five years either, you know, and your split was just as hard on me as it was on you." She patted her daughter's cheek. "We mothers always take on our child's pain as our own." Her tone was long-suffering as she elbowed her way past Lydia and barreled into the apartment, dropping her purse by the front door like she owned the place.

"First of all," Lydia said through clenched teeth, whirling around just as her mother arranged herself neatly on the couch, "Luke is not your son-in-law. We're divorced, remember? And taking baby steps in our relationship to see where it goes. Tonight is our first date. Do you really think it was appropriate for you to come here?"

Cue another wounded look, this time almost comical. "I'm here for moral support, like any good mother. Besides, I was there when you and Luke went on your *actual* first date, wasn't I? If I remember correctly—and I always do—you even asked me to take a picture of the two of you before you left that evening."

"That's because it was the Homecoming dance. And everyone else's parents were there, too, also taking pictures." Lydia's initial anger and annoyance was quickly fading to the bone-weariness she always felt in her mother's presence. Wilma had a larger-than-life personality, and that, combined with her penchant for the dramatic and her uncanny ability to make everything about herself, led Lydia to more or less give up on trying to manage her long ago.

But not tonight. Tonight was about her and Luke, and no one else.

"Leave," she said, opening the door wider and gesturing outside. The sky was beginning to grow dark, a sign of the changing seasons, and a nearby streetlamp ticked on.

Her mother flicked her eyes to the streetlamp, then back to Lydia. "Fine," she said, her tone morose. "But I'll have to walk back—your father's watching the game, and I told him not to come until it's over. You know he won't even hear the phone if I call—his ears are getting worse. And so are mine." She winced as she fingered her earlobes. "Hopefully I'll hear any cars that drive up behind me. And hopefully they'll see me, walking all by myself in the dark, before it's too late." Then she positively hobbled to the door, a far cry from the bounce in her step when she'd strode in moments earlier.

By Lydia's count, her mother had been on the verge of death for the past thirty-two years—and she reminded Lydia of that every chance she got. "Of course, I'll probably have to stop and rest a few times on the sidewalk," she continued, bending down with a moan to grab her purse off the floor. "Because of my ankles. The arthritis, the doctors say it's getting worse. It's okay, though—I could use a good walk tonight. Pretty soon I probably won't be able to walk at all."

"That's the spirit," Lydia said, opening the door an inch wider. "Nothing like fresh air and exercise—

it does the body wonders." Over her mother's head, she saw a pair of headlights sweep onto the street, and her heart stopped. Luke kept a car parked at the harbor lot, as did most residents of Dolphin Bay, where vehicles were largely prohibited, and it was only natural that he would have picked it up before their date tonight.

As the car slowed at the corner, she squinted through the windshield, then released a sigh of relief. It wasn't Luke—she still had time.

"Oh, and did I mention? My back spasms have returned with a vengeance—the chiropractor, bless his heart, promised to do all he could, but he predicts I'll be in a wheelchair in a few years, maybe even bedridden. Then who will take care of me?" Wilma stopped in the doorway, her eyes sweeping over her daughter from head to foot. "You look beautiful, dear. Tell Luke I love him and I'll see him again soon... God willing."

Then she turned around and bumped right into Luke, who had somehow made it almost to Lydia's front door without either woman noticing.

"Oh, *honey*!" Wilma dropped her purse on the sidewalk with a thud and positively launched herself in Luke's direction. She pinched his cheek, then patted the red spot left behind and kissed it with a loud smacking sound that had Lydia checking her apartment's floorboards, wondering if she could somehow disappear beneath them.

"Honey, honey, *honey*." By now, Luke's face was smashed against Wilma's ample bosom as she clutched him to her, rocking back and forth with him in her arms. Then she pulled away from him quite suddenly, pinching his cheek one last time for good measure. "How I missed this handsome *face*!"

She dropped her voice to a not-so-soft whisper. "Lydia's kicking her poor mother out the door. But I told her I had to see you again—I'm so happy the two of you are working things out. You're a gem, honey, a real gem, and it's time my daughter figured that out once and for all."

Lydia's face flamed and she opened her mouth hotly, then decided intervening in this little display wasn't worth her while. Best to let her mother have her say, then usher her out the door with as little fanfare as possible.

Luke met Lydia's eyes over Wilma's shoulders, and the laughter dancing in them was enough to ease her anger. He had always been good with Lydia's mother, knowing just what to say, and precisely how much flattery to add to the mix.

"Mrs. Peterson, I can't tell you how much I've

missed you," he said, obliging her with a quick kiss to the cheek. "I was just telling Lydia last night that I couldn't wait to have dinner at your house again—you make the best cherry pie in the state. I remember you were considering entering it for consideration for the blue ribbon at the state fair a few years back, weren't you?"

"Stop, you flatter me." Wilma shook a playful finger in his face. "And yes, I was, you're such a sweetheart to remember. I didn't get a chance back then, my hip had flared up again, but maybe this is my year. And if it is, you'll be there to cheer me on, won't you?"

"Wild horses couldn't keep me away." This time, when Luke met Lydia's eyes, the meaning behind the words was clear: he was speaking to her, and her alone.

She felt her heart skip a beat as their gazes remained locked. After several long seconds, Luke tore his eyes from hers to address her mother in a tone that Lydia herself had never managed to perfect: warm but stern, friendly while still keeping his distance. "Now if you don't mind, Mrs. Peterson, I've been waiting all day to take Lydia on the perfect date. So if you'll excuse me for now, I'd love to find time for us to catch up later."

"Name the time and I'll be there." Wilma patted his cheek affectionately before lifting her purse from the sidewalk—this time sans moans and groans and imminent death—and sliding it over her shoulder. "And please, honey, call me Mom, just like you used to."

She started to walk away, then stopped and turned, and Lydia was startled to see that her mother's eyes were brimming with tears. "I can't tell you how happy I am to see you two kids back together again. Like I told Lydia a couple weeks ago, you belong with each other. The world just wasn't right when you weren't wearing those wedding rings of yours."

Then she was gone, her heels clip-clopping down the sidewalk as she walked the few blocks to the house she and Lydia's father shared. They watched her in silence for a few moments before Luke turned to Lydia, his eyes drinking her in.

"You look… incredible." He took her hand and spun her in a slow circle, causing Lydia's dress to fan around her. Then he stepped back to take her in once more and gave a low whistle as he shook his head. "I never forgot how beautiful you were, but you've outdone yourself tonight."

"Oh, stop," Lydia said, batting him on the arm

with an embarrassed laugh, then cringing as she realized she sounded exactly like her mother. To cover up the awkward moment, she glanced up and down the street, looking for a car. "I didn't even see you drive up—where did you park?"

"I didn't." Luke shrugged. "Your place is only a five-minute walk from the ferry, so I figured I could use the fresh air. Get rid of some of that nervous energy." He grinned at her, and it struck her for the first time that he was probably feeling just as awkward about the evening as she was. Which was ridiculous, she thought, because they'd been on more dates over the years than she could count.

Still, how many women could say they were excited to be out for a romantic evening with their ex-husband?

"So..." Lydia said as Luke raked a nervous hand through his hair. "Do you want to come in?"

He raised one eyebrow, head cocked slightly, a slow-burn smile on his lips she could feel in her very skin. "Why Ms. Showalter, are you inviting me into your apartment on our first date? How very forward." Grinning, he held out an arm. "Luckily for you, I'm a gentleman. And I would never dream of accepting such an offer."

She took his arm, and they strolled together

down the sidewalk, heading toward the row of restaurants that lined the harbor street, overlooking the glittering water and, somewhere in the distance, the island Lydia had once called home. They chatted as they walked, the conversation shifting from their respective jobs to memories from their teen years, when they'd lived and played and loved on Dolphin Bay.

"Do you remember the senior prank you and Mark Donatello played on our last day of high school?" Lydia said, tears of laughter already swimming in her eyes at the memory. "With the pigs?"

"How could I forget that?" Luke's face split into a wide smile. "His uncle was a farmer on the mainland, and he somehow convinced him to send two of his best pigs over on the ferry. We made a little saddle for each one, with 'Pig 1' and 'Pig 3' written on them." By now, he had started laughing so hard he had to stop walking, releasing Lydia's arm as they both doubled over and strangers in the street sidestepped them, watching the two with amusement.

"They looked for 'Pig 2' for a solid week—tore the whole school apart and never could find him," Luke said, gasping for breath. They both took a few moments to compose themselves before linking arms again and continuing down the road, walking closer together this time.

"We had a lot of fun, didn't we?" Luke said quietly as they stopped at a crosswalk opposite the harbor. The lights from the streetlamps glowed across the water's surface, stretching far into the distance.

"We did," Lydia acknowledged. After that, they both fell silent, lost in thought, and Lydia suspected they were wondering the same thing. Where had it all gone wrong?

The "walk" sign lit up green, and Luke wrapped his arm around her waist as they crossed the road. The harbor was bustling this evening, and a blend of sounds hit their ears as they approached the water: the quiet conversation of diners enjoying a meal and the view at the outdoor tables that lined the street, laughter pouring out from a nearby karaoke bar, a solo jazz musician under a streetlamp, his instrument case open to accept tips, the melancholy notes of his song drifting over the water. They stopped and listened to him for a while, Luke holding her close, and before they stepped away, he slipped a five-dollar bill into the man's case, receiving a nod of thanks in acknowledgement of the gesture.

They wandered down the street for a time, perusing the menus set up on stands outside each restaurant's front door, before choosing an Italian eatery that was slightly off the main road. Only a few diners were inside, speaking in hushed tones as a trio of violinists played in the corner, and the tuxedoed waiters bustled around, arms weighed down with dishes of pasta and squares of creamy tiramisu that had Lydia's mouth watering.

Luke pulled out her chair before taking his own seat opposite her, and after ordering a bottle of red wine for them to share, he closed the drinks menu and steepled his fingers beneath his chin as he stared at her intently, his eyes glittering in the soft overhead lighting. "So," he said, "what should we talk about? Other than how absolutely stunning you look tonight. But I've said that a few times already, and I suspect you're starting to get sick of hearing it."

"Oh, I'm not sure a woman ever gets sick of hearing such things," she replied coyly, taking a sip from her water glass, eyes never leaving his face. "So feel free to tell me again."

Luke gave a soft laugh, and then they shared a smile, intimate and filled with promise. The violinists chose that moment to approach their table, and Lydia reached for his hand as they played a beautiful melody just for them. When the men had finished, bowing before moving on to the next table, the waiter delivered their caprese salad appetizer, a favorite of theirs that they had shared many times over the years.

"Something my mother said got me thinking," Lydia said, resuming their conversation after taking a bite of tomato and wiping a drop of balsamic from her lips. "She said the world hadn't been right since we last wore our wedding rings. Where do you keep yours, anyway? I assume you haven't worn it since… well, since our last day together." Lydia felt a wave of sadness at the memory, but did her best to push it aside—tonight wasn't about the past; it was about the present… and hopefully, the future.

She noticed that Luke's face blanched, which immediately set the alarm bells ringing. Releasing his hand, Lydia pressed her fingers over her mouth and said, "You didn't sell it, did you?" To think that he could so callously part with something that had once meant the world to both of them made Lydia feel numb. But did she have a right to feel that way? She had, after all, given him every reason to think those rings meant nothing.

Her eyes filled with tears, and she glanced down, eyes on her lap as she dabbed at the corners of them with her napkin.

"I didn't sell the ring," Luke said quietly, and

when she looked back up again, she noticed that the couple at the next table were watching them curiously. The woman gave her a sympathetic smile before returning her attention to her husband, and Lydia's cheeks burned with embarrassment.

Dabbing at her eyes one last time—and feeling silly for jumping to conclusions in the first place—Lydia sniffed and said, "I'm glad to hear that." She gave him a watery smile that he failed to return; instead, his lips were pursed and he was staring at her intently, as if debating whether or not to speak. "What?" she asked warily.

Luke ran his fingers idly down his cheeks before cupping them beneath his chin, pressing his mouth to his fingertips for several long moments. Then he winced and said, "I knew this was going to come up at some point, of course, but I was hoping it wouldn't be tonight." He took a deep breath. "I don't have my wedding ring anymore, Lydia. I…" He hesitated, studying her face for a reaction as he said, "I threw it into the ocean."

"You *what*?"

The couple at the neighboring table had dropped all pretenses of not eavesdropping and were now watching them openly. Lydia wasn't sure whether to be horrified, or angry, or deeply, deeply sad at

Luke's revelation. "Why would you do such a thing?"

"Why would I *not* do such a thing?" Luke laughed, though the expression never reached his eyes. She saw the tension in his body as he angled himself toward her, trying without success to shield them from prying eyes. When he spoke next, his voice was barely above a whisper.

"Barely a week ago, you told me you didn't love me, that things were over between us. And that was on top of what you had done all those years ago. So you'll excuse me if I thought the relationship was over. Throwing that ring into the sea was my way of saying goodbye to my past life and trying to cobble together some kind of happy future for myself."

Lydia could see him then, standing on the shoreline, the waves lapping against his ankles as he drew his arm back and launched something into the sea. It had happened right before she'd approached him on the beach that day; hadn't she seen something gold glittering against the sky before it disappeared into the waves? She'd meant to ask him about it, but moments later, when they had kissed, all thoughts of anything but him had melted from her mind.

Luke's expression was cool now; distant. He shot the couple beside them an annoyed look, then focused his attention on his plate, using a butter knife to saw off a bite of mozzarella, basil, and tomato with much more vigor than was necessary, his face intense.

It struck Lydia then that no matter how much he told her that all was forgiven… it wasn't. Beneath the easy smile and the words of adoration was a hurt that ran deep; deeper, perhaps, than either of them realized.

"You know what?" Luke said suddenly, jolting her attention back to his face. "Why don't we forget about all of this for now, okay? This is our first date, and I, for one, want to enjoy it."

Then he grinned at her and stuffed a bite of food into his mouth, washing it down with half the glass of red wine the waiter had poured for him earlier. For the next few minutes—and indeed, the rest of the evening—Luke kept up an easygoing, friendly, and flirtatious banter that would have fooled anyone into thinking he was happy.

But Lydia knew him well enough to recognize the truth.

He wasn't.

CHAPTER 8

"Okay, which one of you lovely ladies is my bride?" The sales associate graced Laurie and Karina with a bright smile as she swung her head back and forth between the two of them while Edie tried to keep a straight face. She couldn't blame the woman for her mistake; after all, how many blushing brides in their seventies could she have possibly met?

"That would be me." Edie waggled her fingers in a dainty wave as her daughters laughed and the sales associate's eyes widened in surprise. She pointed to the beautiful ring Henry had slipped on her finger when he had gotten down on one knee and asked her to be his wife. "If you need any further proof," she said playfully, holding out her hand as though she were a queen waiting for a kiss.

The woman's eyes sparkled with amusement as she clasped Edie's hand briefly in her own. "Then allow me to congratulate you on your wonderful news." Then she straightened up again, still smiling. "My name is Clara, and I'll be helping you find the perfect dress for your big day."

She gestured toward the racks of gowns lining the elegant bridal boutique Edie's daughters had insisted on taking her to. "We have a number of beautiful styles to choose from. Have you had a chance to take a peek at any of our selection yet?"

"No, I wouldn't even know where to start." Edie tugged her shawl around her shoulders, suddenly feeling self-conscious as she gazed at the mannequins displayed around the store, each wearing a stunning gown of white or ivory. She'd always considered herself to be stylish, refusing to fall victim to the frumpy clothes and sensible shoes expected of most women her age, but right now, she felt completely out of her element.

"I have a couple of things in mind that would be perfect for you," Clara said. "Just give me a few minutes and I'll bring over some things for you to try on." She opened one of the dressing rooms and turned on the light, then bent down to arrange a large, round platform in front of a full-length mirror opposite the women. "Before I get started, can I bring you ladies anything to drink? Tea, champagne?"

"Champagne would be fabulous." Laurie raised her hand as Karina nodded along enthusiastically. "What?" she said in response to her mother's look of amusement. "Today is girls' day out. Something that is exceedingly rare when you have too many kids to count running around at home."

"I second that," Karina said happily. "And after this, we're going to that new French restaurant for lunch. Our treat, of course," she said, nudging her sister in the hip.

"My goodness, what special treatment. I guess I need to get engaged every day!" Edie teased, then smiled at Clara. "Nothing for me, please. I have to admit, I'm a little nervous to try on wedding dresses —not only did I never think I'd be in this position again, but I don't exactly have the same body I did when I got married the first time around." She thought back to the gown she'd married Johnny in, with a cathedral-length train and lace that seemed to stretch on for miles. It was a fairytale gown for what had been a fairytale marriage, a love that was cut far too short.

"You're beautiful," Karina said fiercely as Laurie murmured her agreement. She turned to Clara. "We need to find my mother a dress that shows her just how stunning she really is."

"And one that knocks Henry right off his feet," Laurie added, earning a dubious look from Edie.

"Careful what you wish for," she warned. "That stubborn old goat is insisting on leaving his cane at home so we can have a proper first dance. I have a feeling my dress won't be the only thing that leaves him flat on his back."

The three women shared a laugh, and Clara bustled off to pour the champagne, returning a few moments later with two glasses before heading to a row of dresses at the very back corner of the boutique. She was soon hidden from view amid the lace and tulle, and while they waited, Edie's daughters sipped their champagne and perused the gowns hanging on the rack nearest them.

"Look how dreamy this one is," Laurie said with a sigh as she showed the other two an ivory gown with a fitted bodice and an intricate lace design on the full skirt. "I may ask Owen for a divorce just so I can marry him all over again in *this*." She slid the hanger off the rack and held the gown up to her body, admiring her reflection in the mirror. "It's a dress fit for a princess."

She set it back on the rack as they heard Clara's footsteps approaching, and as the sales associate rounded a mannequin, they could see she was carrying three zippered dress bags behind her back. "Here we go," she said, hanging the gowns inside the dressing room. Then she returned to usher Edie inside. "If you need any help, let me know. I'll give you three a few moments to yourself."

The bell above the boutique's door chimed, and a young woman stepped in, accompanied by her mother, both gazing around in wonder at the stunning dresses on display. Clara left to greet them, and Laurie and Karina settled themselves into their chairs, their expressions eager as Edie stepped inside the dressing room and unwound her shawl from her shoulders.

Excitement welled inside her as she fingered the zipper on the first garment bag, trying to imagine Henry's face as he saw her walking down the aisle on Reed's arm. He was a man of few words, but she knew his emotions ran deep—and their wedding day meant more to him than he would ever be able to express. As visions of tulle danced in her head, Edie unzipped the bag, her heart rate quickening with excitement as she opened it to reveal…

A women's suit.

The fabric was a beautiful off-white color with hints of soft pink woven through it, and the coat had intricate beading and beautiful lace detail, but no amount of design work could conceal the fact that it was a simple jacket and knee-length skirt. Fitting for a bride of a certain age, as Edie certainly was. On the outside, at least.

And a quick unzipping of the remaining two bags revealed similar gowns. If you could call them that.

"Mom, I… you look beautiful." Karina's face fell as Edie stepped out of the dressing room, but she was quick to hide her disappointment behind a bright smile. "That color looks absolutely lovely on you." She set down her champagne glass and stood to give Edie a hand as she stepped onto the platform in front of the mirror. "What do you think?"

"It's nice," Edie said, turning in a slow circle to examine the outfit from all angles. "It's certainly comfortable." She faced the mirror and clasped her hands in front of her waist, trying to imagine a bouquet of flowers in them. Trying to imagine that she looked like a bride.

In the mirror's reflection, she saw her daughters

exchange skeptical looks. "You don't like it?" she asked, turning to them. They immediately straightened up, eyes on her.

"Mom, you look beautiful," Laurie said. "That color is just lovely on you—it really brings out your eyes." She slid a glance toward the dressing room. "Did Clara bring anything else you might like to show us?"

"More of the same." Edie sighed and returned her attention to the mirror. "I guess women of my age are expected to look a certain way on their wedding day."

"Says who?" Karina said in an annoyed tone. She waved her champagne glass at her mother's reflection. "I'm not saying you don't look great, Mom... but is this what *you* had envisioned? This is your day, and we want to make sure everything is perfect for you."

Edie tapped her chin, considering her daughter's words. "Marrying Henry will make it a perfect day, but if I'm being perfectly honest..." She glanced at Clara and lowered her voice, a mischievous smile playing across her lips. "I wanted to look a little less frumpy on one of the biggest days of my life."

"I'll take care of that." Karina set her glass down on the table with a *clink* that drew Clara's attention to them, but Edie merely gave her a smile and wave to indicate that everything was okay. Once the sales associate resumed her conversation with the younger bride, Karina set off for the nearest rack of dresses, flipping through them expertly until she said, "Ah-ha!" and unhooked a gown from the rack.

"*This* is what you need." She held out the gown, allowing the fabric to flow over her outstretched arms.

Edie sucked in a breath as she took in the gown's stunning lace bodice, white overlayed on a deep ivory. It had three-quarter-length sleeves, an off-the-shoulder neckline, and a simple A-line silhouette that she suspected would complement her figure well. The gown ended in a short train, and was light enough to be worn at the seaside wedding she and Henry were planning.

"I love it," she said, fingering the fabric, then giving the simple suit she was wearing another once-over. "Do you really think I could pull it off?"

"This dress was made for you." Laurie jumped to her feet and gently took the gown from her sister's arms, carrying it carefully toward the dressing room. Edie was just about to follow, but stopped short when she noticed Clara marching toward them, her eyes on Laurie, her face set in a tight smile.

"Is there something I can help you with?" she asked, her voice pleasant but stern. "We do ask our customers not to remove the merchandise from the racks on their own, but I would be more than happy to help you make some additional selections." She turned to Edie. "What did you think of the ones I chose for you?"

"We were just picking out a gown we thought would be better suited for our mother," Karina said, pointing at the dress in Laurie's arms. "Something a little more… elegant."

"Oh." Clara looked visibly taken aback. "My apologies if I was off-base; usually our older brides want something less formal, simpler." She glanced at the gown Karina had chosen, her face softening into a smile. "But if you ask me, that one would look absolutely lovely on you. Here, why don't you step into the dressing room and I'll help you slip it on."

As Laurie hung up the gown, Clara held out a hand to escort Edie off the platform. Minutes later, they reemerged from the room, and Edie could tell without looking in the mirror that her face was glowing. The dress fit like a glove—it wouldn't even need alterations. The fabric felt like velvet against her skin, and the gown was lightweight enough that she and Henry would be able to dance the night away—well, she would, anyway, Edie thought with a smile as Clara helped her step back onto the platform.

When Edie saw her reflection for the first time, she couldn't stop the tears from springing to her eyes. "Oh, Mom," Karina whispered, digging around in her purse for a tissue that she used to dab at her own eyes. Beside her, Laurie was beaming. "It's perfect. It's absolutely perfect."

"Well?" Clara asked, stepping to the side, arms folded in front of her as she grinned at Edie's reflection. "Are you saying yes to the dress?"

"No." Edie shook her head resolutely as her daughters shared a look of confusion. Then she turned around, her eyes shining with happiness. "I'm saying *heck* yes to the dress."

"I CAN'T MOVE. I quite literally cannot spend one more second on my feet today." Daphne dropped into the nearest chair, kicked off her shoes, and rubbed her feet, wincing as she glanced up at Jax, who looked about as exhausted as she felt. The past two days had been a blur—an amazing, exciting, thrilling blur, but a blur all the same.

"I feel you. I'm pretty sure I could sleep for a week." The purple shadows under Jax's eyes were highlighted in the bakery's overhead lighting as he pulled out the chair across from Daphne and sank into it. He rubbed a hand over his face as he took in Sugarbloom's display cases, empty save for a couple of chocolate chip cookies and a lone cupcake. Rising to his feet with a groan, he slid open the case, grabbed the leftover treats, and returned, setting them down on the table between them.

"I didn't even get a chance to stop for a quick bite to eat," Daphne said, eyeing the cupcake longingly. Jax split it down the middle, then offered half to her, along with a cookie. "Thanks," she said, digging in. They chewed in silence for a few moments, both gazing out at the darkening sky. In the distance, the ocean was glittering like a thousand diamonds as the streetlamps clicked on and the island's ferry cut through the gentle waves.

Daphne watched it all with a sense of awe, not just at the beautiful surroundings, but awe at what had taken place inside her humble bakery over the past two days. She had always known that Dolphin Bay was a warm, welcoming town whose residents treated everyone—neighbors and strangers alike—as though they were family. It was one of the things she loved best about living here, one of the reasons why she could never picture herself anywhere else. But the amount of support they'd shown her, the way they'd helped make her dreams come true... it was far more than she could ever repay them for.

Not a minute had gone by when the bakery was empty. Daphne had been working in the kitchen round the clock to keep up with the demand, while a rotating circle of friends, including Jax, Tana, and Reed, had taken shifts at the counter as their own work schedules permitted. She couldn't be more grateful to them for their help, Jax in particular; he had gone above and beyond what anyone could ever ask for, and he had done it all with a smile on his face.

The customers loved him, too; Daphne noticed more than one woman light up as he boxed up their treats, his friendly, easygoing manner shining through despite how exhausted she knew he must be. One woman, younger than Daphne by about ten years, with long, wavy hair and big blue eyes, had lingered at one of the bakery's tables long after she had finished her slice of pie, and Daphne had to resist the urge to give her the stink eye.

Not only would that have been bad for business,

of course, but also... she had no claim over Jax. Not anymore.

She studied his profile now as he gazed out at the water, watching a couple of kids pack up their sand toys for the evening, wrapping thick beach towels around themselves to ward off the chill that had settled in the air. A feeling of emptiness settled in the pit of her stomach. A sense of loss, even though he was sitting right beside her.

"I have an idea," he said, turning quite suddenly away from the window, leaving Daphne with barely enough time to glance away before he noticed her eyes on him. "Why don't we have a barbecue on the beach tonight, like old times? I'm sure my uncle has one of those portable grills around the inn somewhere—when I was a kid, I remember several of the guests asking to borrow one. It's a perfect night for it and—"

He was interrupted when his cell phone rang, vibrating on the table between them. As Jax glanced at the caller ID, an unreadable expression settled over his face before he picked up the phone and slid his finger over the screen to answer the call.

"Jax Keller here."

Daphne could only hear one side of the conversation, but the deep, booming sound of Steve

Neuman's voice was instantly recognizable, even at a distance.

She felt her lungs constricting as Jax's hand tightened around the phone; he was listening so intently to the other man that he didn't seem to notice he was holding his breath. But Daphne saw it—and she saw, too, the look of excitement, of anticipation, that crossed his face a moment later.

"Yes, we'll talk again soon, figure out the rest of the details. And thank you again for the call. Uh-uh. Great. Okay, I'll see you then."

Jax hung up the phone, then lowered it to the table, staring at the blank screen with an expression of disbelief. Then, slowly, he raised his gaze to Daphne, his blue-green eyes sparkling. "I did it," he breathed, his voice barely above a whisper. "I got the job."

A moment of silence followed, and then he suddenly let out a whoop and jumped to his feet, then rounded the table and grabbed Daphne by the hands. He pulled her up from her chair and wrapped his arms around her in a massive bear hug; she clung to him, tears wetting her eyelashes, face turned into his chest so he wouldn't see.

"Daphne, I can't believe it—can you believe it?" Jax pulled away from her and raked his hands through his hair, then clutched the ends of it, shaking his head in wonder. He let out another laugh, throwing his head back to the ceiling; somewhere outside, a seagull cried overhead, as if echoing his excitement.

Then he exhaled a long, deep breath and steadied himself against the nearest display case, still shaking his head. "Oh, Daph—you don't know what this means to me right now. A few months ago, I thought my career, everything I've worked so hard for, was over. And now… I'm being given an opportunity that most chefs would kill for."

He reached for her hands once more. "Thank you. I couldn't have pulled off that tasting without you."

Daphne laughed, then quickly looked away, busying herself by heading for the nearest table and sweeping the crumbs from it into her open palm. "Thanks for the flattery, but I didn't do anything but set the plates in front of him. You would have gotten the job with or without me." She glanced up, meeting his gaze for the first time. "Congratulations, Jax," she said warmly, and meant it. Because he deserved every amazing opportunity that came his way.

"Wow. Wow wow wow." Jax cupped both hands over his mouth, then laughed again. "Miami Beach, here I come." He grinned at her. "Now we *definitely* need to have that beach barbecue tonight. Between the two of us, we have a heck of a lot to celebrate."

"Sounds great." Daphne gave him as enthusiastic a smile as she could muster before dumping the crumbs into the trash can and moving on to the next table. Her excitement about the bakery's success was dimming further with each passing moment, and as Jax positively bounced out the door in search of a grill for the evening's festivities, she couldn't help but wonder whether only one of them would truly be celebrating tonight.

CHAPTER 9

"I just wanted to thank you for a memorable stay. My husband and I had a wonderful time, and we're already planning to come back around the holidays for a little winter getaway. Will you still be open in December?"

"Absolutely." Tana smiled up at the couple, the latest of the inn's guests who were headed back home. "And you couldn't choose a better spot for a weekend getaway around the holidays. The island is simply stunning in the winter, and I'm a decorating fiend—so you can expect more lights and wreaths and Christmas trees than you'll find at Santa's workshop."

She shared a laugh with the couple, who spent a few more minutes complimenting the newly renovated inn as Tana collected their keys and settled the bill. Only when they said goodbye and headed for the door with promises to see her again soon did Tana notice that Reed was standing just inside the foyer, face lit up with a grin.

"They couldn't have had better things to say about the inn," he said, stepping forward to greet her with a kiss. "You should be feeling pretty good about yourself right now."

"I'm feeling pretty good about Uncle Henry and the inn," she corrected him with a smile, then beckoned him over to the computer. "Here. Take a look at this." A few clicks of the mouse, and the inn's booking calendar came into view. Each date that could no longer accept reservations was grayed out, and Tana had woken that morning to a sea of gray.

Reed gave a low whistle as he bent over the computer. "Seems like the article in the *Maine Herald* brought you plenty of attention. I'm sure word of mouth is helping, too—hey." He frowned as he leaned further over the computer, squinting as he studied the screen. "These names... I recognize at least two-thirds of them." He scratched his chin, raising his eyes to Tana. "They're all people who live on the island."

"I know." Not for the first time since she'd seen

the reservation list that morning, Tana's eyes welled up with tears of happiness and gratitude. "Obviously our neighbors have no reason to book a stay at the inn, other than to show Henry their support." She shook her head. "Between this and what I've seen at Daphne's bakery over the past couple of days... I can't believe how kind people are in Dolphin Bay. I've never experienced anything like it before."

"We always take care of our own," Reed said, still scrolling through the list. Then he straightened up and glanced down the hallway at Uncle Henry's closed bedroom door. "Have you told him about it yet?"

"No." Tana closed the calendar with a click of the mouse. "He and Edie are out doing some wedding thing or another—it's hard to keep up with them these days."

"Yeah, she's been running around like a chicken with her head cut off," Reed said with a chuckle. "Both of my sisters, too. I'm doing my best to stay out of it, and not give my opinion unless I'm specifically asked to. I made the grievous error of suggesting hot dogs and hamburgers for the wedding dinner and Laurie almost bit my head off. What?" he asked, frowning at Tana when he noticed her gaping at him in disbelief. "It's a *beach* wedding. What else would you serve?"

"Remind me not to ask for your help either if we ever get—" She stopped speaking abruptly when she realized what she'd been about to say.

"Go on." Reed gave her a sly smile. "Why don't you finish that thought."

"Never mind." Tana's cheeks were flaming as she busied herself shuffling and reshuffling random stacks of paperwork that she grabbed from the inn's desk. What in the world had possessed her to almost say something like that? She and Reed were in a happy, fulfilling relationship, sure, but the topic of marriage? That had certainly never come up. And not just because Tana was still technically married to someone else.

"It's okay to be shy." Reed's smile was growing more wicked by the second. "Luckily for you, I'm not, so I'll go right ahead and finish that thought for you." He leaned over the desk, his face inches from hers. "If we ever get married." Then he leaned in closer, until their lips were practically brushing. "Only there's one problem with that sentence."

"Oh?" Tana cocked her head at him. "And what would that be?"

"You should have said *when* we get married."

Reed's pale blue eyes met hers. "Because believe me, it's going to happen."

"Is it?" Tana was practically whispering now as her heart hammered away, threatening to burst right out of her chest. "You sound awfully confident about that." She glanced down at her left hand and then back up again. "Seems to me there's no ring on my finger."

Reed smiled, slow and teasing, and Tana's stomach flipped. "Not today." He reached forward, fingertips brushing the end of her long hair, eyes latched onto hers. Tana cupped her hands around his face and drew his mouth to hers, and the kiss they shared was long and leisurely and filled with promise.

"Can't you do that somewhere else? Some people are trying to eat lunch here." Tana and Reed broke their kiss and looked up to find Jax and Emery watching them in amusement, both holding a plate containing a sandwich, chips, and an apple. Jax took an enormous bite of his apple and chewed it slowly as he looked pointedly in Reed's direction. "I don't remember giving you permission to put your mitts on my sister."

"And I don't remember giving *you* permission to eat those chips. You know they're my favorite." Tana tugged the plate out of his hands, ignoring his protests, and popped several chips into her mouth while Emery shook her head.

"Whenever I'm around the two of you, I feel like I'm the adult and you're the kids."

Tana laughed. "Being on the island makes me feel like a kid again—it brings me right back to those days that your Uncle Jax and I spent here. Those were the kinds of summers you read about in books and see in movies—just the two of us, our bicycles, and the sea."

"Speaking of how our mother shipped us off to Dolphin Bay each year without a second thought," Jax said, his eyes turning stormy, "did you manage to get in touch with her? Uncle Henry told me he was really hoping she'd be at the wedding."

"No." Tana's heart sank as she remembered her uncle's expression when he'd asked her to get in touch with Julie, how he considered her the daughter he never had. "Not for lack of trying, though. I've called her several times and left voicemails, but you know Mom… she'll get back to me when she's good and ready. She has that big job opportunity this summer photographing the wildlife in the national parks. If I know her, right now she's camped out in a pine tree in Alaska, trying to get the perfect shot of a grizzly bear."

"Yeah, well, I hope you never hear back from her." Jax's face was set in stone. "As far as I'm concerned, she's done nothing to help Uncle Henry these past few months, and doesn't deserve to be a guest at his wedding."

Tana sighed, silently acknowledging the truth behind her brother's words but also knowing that he was coming from a place of hurt. Julie's lack of mothering had affected Jax deeply as a child, an untended wound that had only grown more difficult for him to heal as an adult. Maybe what the two of them needed was a chance to sit down and talk.

Or maybe what they needed was for Julie to continue holding her two children at arm's length, for reasons Tana would never understand. But her own childhood experiences had prompted her to be the best mother she could, and if she never did anything else of note in her life, that would always be enough.

The front door opened and Edie stepped inside, followed closely by Henry, who navigated the porch steps with some difficulty before sinking onto a chair in the inn's foyer. "Flowers are all picked out!" Edie announced. "And Henry had a fitting today for his tuxedo—the man actually looks sophisticated for once in his life." She gave him an affectionate smile, then caught sight of the others' faces. "What's going on in here? You could cut the tension with a knife."

"We're just arguing about the best type of food to serve on your big day," Reed stepped in smoothly, walking forward to greet his mother with a quick kiss on the cheek. "My vote is the same, and I think I've managed to convince a few of the others to join my team."

"Reed Dawes, if you suggest I serve my guests hot dogs one more time, I'll send you to your room without dinner." She shook a finger in his face, and Reed's booming laughter caused the tension to bleed out of Tana's body. A sideways glance at her brother showed that he, too, looked more relaxed, although she had a feeling their conversation was far from over. Still, now wasn't the time to discuss Julie, especially in Henry's presence, so Tana decided a much happier subject was in order.

"Guess what?" she said, turning to Henry, who eyed her with apprehension.

"What?"

"There's something I want to show you." She beckoned for Edie and Henry to join her behind the desk, offering her uncle the chair before switching on the computer and navigating to the inn's reservation calendar.

Her uncle swept his eyes over it, lips pursed, then tipped his face up to Tana. "You know I don't know anything about this technology mumbo-jumbo. Just what am I looking at here?"

Tana laughed at the sound of the old man's ornery tone. Some things never changed. "What you're looking at," she said gently, "is the inn's reservation list for the next two months. All these days here"—she pointed to the screen, indicating the gray blocks on the calendar—"are already fully booked."

"Fully booked?" Henry squinted at her as if he didn't understand what she was telling him. "As in..."

"As in there's no room left at the inn," Jax said, grinning down at his uncle from his spot over Tana's shoulder.

Edie, like her son before her, was studying the computer screen, silently mouthing the names on the reservation list while Tana and Reed shared a knowing smile over her head.

"Henry, this is..." Edie lowered her face closer to the screen, as if still not believing what she was seeing. "This is half the island!" She pressed her fingers to her mouth, her eyes tearing up as she swept her gaze between Tana and Reed. "All these people coming to support him. It's overwhelming."

As the others began talking over each other, discussing this exciting turn of events, Henry alone sat silent, his faded green eyes still fixed on the screen. When Tana noticed this, she bent down beside him until they were shoulder to shoulder and whispered, "What do you think, Uncle Henry?"

Her uncle didn't respond, but he didn't have to. The handkerchief he retrieved from his pocket to dab at the corners of his eyes told her everything she needed to know.

MANY HOURS LATER, when night had fallen over the island and the inn was still and silent, Tana sat in front of the computer, mug of tea at her side, and stared at the screen, her eyes straining to read the small text in the darkness. She had been scrolling through website after website for hours, and as she read and discarded each entry on the screen, she could feel her stomach sinking further toward her feet.

"You're up late." Jax padded into the inn's foyer from the kitchen, glass of water in hand, eyes bleary from exhaustion and hair sticking up in every direction. "Everything okay?"

Tana considered her response for a few moments, then ultimately sighed and shook her head. "No, everything is definitely not okay."

"Is it Reed?" Jax's eyebrows shot up in alarm as he closed the distance between himself and his sister. "Did something happen between the two of you?"

"No," Tana said adamantly. "That's the only part of my life that doesn't feel like it's in freefall—my relationship with him." She smiled softly, then caught sight of the screen again and heaved another sigh. "I'm just trying to figure out my next steps, and I'm coming up empty."

"Ah. The unknowns of the future. I could tell you a thing or two about that." Jax leaned against the desk, sipping his water and eyeing her over the rim of his glass. "I take it you've noticed that Uncle Henry is getting spryer by the day."

"And more eager to get back into the swing of things," Tana added, leaning back in the desk chair and rubbing her eyes, which were grainy from exhaustion. "He doesn't have to say it, but I can tell. Every day he takes on just a little bit more than the day before. Pretty soon—sooner than I probably want to admit—I'll be handing the reins back over to him completely."

She smiled, though the expression held more than a hint of sadness. "As it should be, of course. This beautiful place"—she swept her arm around the foyer—"isn't just part of Uncle Henry. It *is* Uncle Henry."

Jax took another sip of water, his face contemplative as he considered her words. "I don't know about that," he said after a long pause.

Tana frowned at him. "What do you mean?"

Stepping away from the desk, Jax ran his fingers along the inn's walls. "This inn *used* to be Uncle Henry. But now—don't you think it's a part of all of us? Each of us has had a hand in its success, and each of us loves it—maybe not as much as Uncle Henry, but that doesn't mean it's not ours just the same."

Tana was quiet for a long moment after that, considering all the ways the inn—and her uncle—had changed over the past few months. "Maybe you're right," she murmured, eyes drifting around the room. "But that still doesn't mean it's not time for me to step away. Soon, anyway."

"No," Jax acknowledged. "It doesn't. But it means that you aren't saying goodbye to the inn—you're saying..." He scrunched his nose in thought as he tried to figure out the right word. "Well, I'm not sure what you're saying," he said finally with a laugh. "But I know one thing for sure—it *isn't* goodbye."

He yawned widely, stretching his arms over his head. "As for your next move, I think you have some time before you need to figure that out. That computer screen is straining my eyes in this darkness, and I'm not even the one looking at it. Why don't you call it a night?"

Tana's gaze wandered back over to the screen, where an endless list of search results awaited her. She'd been researching possible career choices, along with available jobs in and around Dolphin Bay, but had come up empty… and worried. While Derek's Hollywood career had left her with plenty of money, between what she had put toward the inn's renovations and what she would need to find a new home once she was no longer living at the inn, that money wasn't infinite. Eventually, she would need a paycheck—and not just for the money. For a way to take pride in herself, in her abilities, and forge the kind of life for herself she had always imagined.

But was she really going to figure all of that out tonight?

"You're right," Tana said, leaning forward and switching off the screen, watching as the picture faded to black. She rose and rounded the desk, then slung an arm over her brother's shoulders as they began walking back to their respective rooms. "I could always join you in Miami Beach," she teased.

She expected one of her brother's witty responses, but he was uncharacteristically silent for several long beats. When he noticed her watching him from the corner of her eye, he laughed… just a little too loud. "Yeah," he said. "Between the two of us, we'd really tear up the town."

Then he yawned widely again, one hand covering his mouth. "I'm beat. I'm gonna hit the sack." He leaned over and pressed a brotherly kiss to the top of her head. "You get some sleep too, okay? Between the inn, the bakery, and the wedding, we all have our plates way too full. Sooner or later, it's going to catch up with us."

Then he patted her on the arm and nudged open his bedroom door, disappearing inside and closing it behind him with a soft *click*.

Tana's gaze lingered on the door for a moment before she tiptoed away, heading for her own room—and the soft bed that awaited. Jax was right: things were definitely starting to catch up with her. With a soft moan of exhaustion, she lowered herself onto the covers, not even bothering to kick off her shoes, and allowed her head to sink into the pillow. Moments later, her thoughts began drifting into dreams, her body relaxing deeper into the bed, until the silence was shattered by the insistent ringing of her cell phone.

She fumbled for it, her mind instantly alert as she remembered Emery was still out for the evening with some locals her own age she had been spending time with in recent days. Her daughter may technically be an adult, with all the rights and responsibilities that came with it, but to Tana, she was her forever baby, the girl who lit up her life in ways she could never even begin to explain. A glance at the unfamiliar number on the screen only amplified her fears, and so it was in a guarded voice that Tana answered the phone, clicking on the bedside lamp and bathing her room in an orange glow.

"Tana? Is that you?" The line was staticky, but the familiar voice broke through it all the same.

Tana instantly felt herself relaxing. Not Emery.

"Mom? I mean Julie?" She squinted at the small clock on the nightstand. It was nearing one in the morning. "Why are you calling me so late? Is everything okay?"

"Everything's fine," her mother said with a laugh. "I just forgot the time difference, that's all. I'm in

Yellowstone. Would you believe I've spent the past three weeks trying to track down a pack of wolverines? Every time I think I'm getting close, those darn things outsmart me again. But *National Geographic* is desperate for pictures of them—they're masters at evading people—and so I'm doing my best to deliver."

As Tana listened to her mother, she had to resist the urge to sigh. They hadn't spoken for, what? Four months? Not since Julie found out about Tana's divorce. And here she was, spouting off about her job, as usual. Not a second to spare to ask how Tana might be, or Jax, or heaven forbid Uncle Henry, who was still recovering from a life-threatening stroke.

Stop it. Tana inhaled slowly, letting her anger cool on the exhale that followed. This was who her mother was; nothing—and no one—was going to change that. She had made peace with that fact years ago; well, as much peace as she could, anyway. Some hurts always lingered just beneath the skin.

"Anywho," her mother was saying as Tana tuned back into the conversation. "I got your messages about the wedding, but I haven't had a chance to call you back. Now I've gone and lost my cell phone—I'm as brainless as ever." She chuckled. "So I'm calling you from the front desk at the lodge where I'm staying. And the answer is yes."

Tana frowned, trying to make sense of Julie's last words. "Yes what?"

"Yes, I will absolutely be at Uncle Henry's wedding," Julie said, her tone mildly impatient. "You know how much I love that old man—I wouldn't miss it for the world."

Tana's eyebrows shot up into her hairline. This was an unexpected turn of events. Then she immediately became suspicious. "Are you sure about that? I don't want to tell him you're coming and then have to take it back."

"Tana." Her mother sounded wounded. "How could you think a thing like that? If I say I'm going to be there, I'm going to be there. Already bought my ticket, in fact. I have it right here." There was a rustling sound on the line. "I'll be flying out the evening before the wedding. Will you pick me up at the airport?" She rattled off the airline, flight number, and times while Tana scrambled for a piece of paper and a pen, jotting them down from memory before tearing off the paper and placing it in her nightstand drawer for safekeeping.

"Okay," she said, "I'll see you then. Uncle Henry

will be thrilled you're coming—he was hoping you would."

"I can't wait to see everyone." The line crackled again, louder this time, and her mother's next words were muffled. All Tana could make out was something that sounded like "miss you" before the static intensified and the line went dead. She stared at the blank screen for several moments, waiting for a return call.

When the phone remained silent, Tana shook her head, then flipped off the light and slipped into bed.

CHAPTER 10

"Are you ready for this?" Lydia asked her reflection as she stared at herself in her car's rearview mirror. She had been sitting in the parking lot assigned to the Dolphin Bay ferry for the past two hours, long before she was set to sail out from the mainland. Normally, she would have walked, but her nerves were getting the better of her; her legs had felt like jelly for the better part of the morning, and it was all she could do to get through a wedding dress fitting, venue walk-through, and two potential client interviews without falling apart completely. Her job, like any, was stressful. But there was something almost poetically awful about dealing with starry-eyed brides when she was terrified about the state of her own relationship.

How had they gotten back here already? To the stiffness, the awkwardness, the general discomfort with being in each other's presence? Wasn't their reunion—and their love—supposed to fix all of that?

Only in fairytales, Lydia thought with a sigh. When she and Luke had kissed on the beach all those days ago, she knew they were in for a long, hard road to recovery, to finding their place with each other again. But now that the real work was about to start, now that the glossy newness was fading, the cracks were beginning to emerge.

She had hurt Luke deeply, more deeply than either one of them cared to admit. For that, she took full responsibility. But would he ever truly be able to forgive her? He said yes, but during their first date, when the subject had come up, his eyes… they told a different story. And that story had broken Lydia's heart all over again.

"You're awfully quiet," Kurt said forty-five minutes later when Lydia had boarded the ferry and settled into a seat beside the railing. The ferry to the island was quiet at this time of day, and also at this time of year, when most of the tourists had packed up their bathing suits and beach chairs and headed back to real life, spending the next nine months dreaming of sunny days and warm, starry nights.

She gave the captain a sad smile. "I have a lot of things on my mind."

"Ah." Kurt glanced at his watch, then propped one leg on the chair beside her, resting his elbows on it and watching her intently. "Need someone to talk to about it? We don't leave for another twenty minutes, and the way things are looking, it's only going to be you and me on this big boat."

He smiled, the sun-leathered skin at the corners of his startlingly blue eyes wrinkling. Kurt had been the ferry's captain going back to Lydia's childhood; he was a Dolphin Bay staple, a man with a ready smile who knew everyone and had never met a stranger. Lydia had always been fond of him, but some topics of discussion needed to stay private.

Just then, a young couple boarded the ferry, holding hands and laughing together, and as she watched them, something inside Lydia broke. Eyes welling up with tears, she fished around in her purse for a tissue while Kurt looked on in concern. "I'm afraid," she admitted. "Luke and I are trying to give things another go, and I'm terrified it won't work. I'm terrified I'll lose him again."

Her eyes drifted to the couple once more; the

man was whispering something into the woman's ear while stroking her windswept hair back from her forehead. The tenderness, the look of absolute love in his eyes… it was almost too much for her to bear. Not so very long ago, Luke had looked at her that way, and they had still managed to make a mess of things.

"I see." Kurt was quiet for a time after that, his eyes never leaving her face. Then he turned his gaze out to the open water, a stormy blue today, echoing the gray clouds that swirled overhead, bringing with them the promise of refreshing rain.

"Love is hard," he said, his eyes on the horizon, where a trio of dolphins were leaping effortlessly in and out of the water. "When you find the person who makes your heart soar, when you know in here"—he thumped his chest—"that you're finally done looking, you think it's all roses and romantic dinners and sunset walks along the shore."

He laughed softly, his silver hair highlighted by a ray of sun that had broken through the clouds. "Then you settle down and you realize it's very little of that, and a whole lot of arguing about whose turn it is to do the laundry, or who put the milk carton back inside the fridge empty, or who has to get up in the middle of the night to feed the baby. And when it's over, when you've lost that person and you think back hard on your time together, you realize that in between those stupid arguments is where the magic happens: the jokes, the laughter, the times when you don't want to see their face again but wouldn't know what to do without them. It may not be the fairytale romance everyone envisions, but it's a different fairytale, one that most people would move mountains to experience just once in their lifetime."

His eyes clouded over with sadness, and Lydia knew he was remembering his wife Lottie, who had passed away several years ago. He turned to her then, his smile haunted. "I'm an old man, so maybe you should take what I'm saying with a grain of salt. Or maybe you shouldn't, for the very same reason. But if you find that person, do what it takes to make it work. You don't want to look back on your life and realize that you spent too much of it being unhappy. Because life is precious, and fleeting, and before we know what happened, in the blink of an eye, our hair is gray and we walk a little slower than we used to."

He rested a hand on her shoulder and gave it a gentle squeeze. "If you love this man, and if he loves you, then sit down together and fix things. You'll never regret it—because there will come a day when what you have now, when the love you share, is nothing more than a memory that you hold onto as tightly as you can, trying to prevent it from slipping away."

He released his hold on Lydia, and then, with a tip of his cap, he made his way toward the captain's station, calling out greetings to the other riders settling in for the trip. She barely paid any attention to her surroundings, dimly aware of the jolt beneath her as the ferry left the harbor and glided through the water, sending seagulls flapping toward the sky with cries of alarm. What seemed like moments later, as she stared out at the approaching island without really seeing it, Kurt had navigated them safely into the Dolphin Bay harbor.

Lydia hadn't expected Luke to meet her, but he was there all the same, standing on the weathered wooden dock, hands in the pockets of his jeans, expression guarded as she disembarked. They hadn't spoken much since their date, both worried about what today would bring, and so he responded with a look of surprise, and then affection, when Lydia threw herself into Luke's arms and held on for dear life.

"Hey, what's all this?" he murmured into her hair as he stroked it. "Is everything okay?"

She pulled away from him, wiping her eyes. "I want things to work out with us. I *need* things to work out with us. I can't lose you—not again."

"Well that's why we're doing this, right?" He waved his hand in the vague direction of town. "Going to therapy."

She couldn't help noticing the tightness around his mouth as he said the word, and she stepped back from him, gazing up into his eyes. "You're not comfortable with this, are you?"

"I'll do anything for you, and you know that," he said, seamlessly sidestepping the question.

Not to be deterred, Lydia said, "But how do *you* feel about it?"

Luke hesitated, his eyes lingering on the other ferry passengers strolling down the ramp, then to the line of people forming at the harbor's edge, waiting patiently to board for their trip to the mainland. "I'm not crazy about sharing such deeply personal things with a stranger, no. But I'm willing to try—if it's something you want, then it's something I want."

He slipped his hand into hers, and together they began walking up the dirt path leading to town.

There was only one therapist living on the island, a woman in her thirties named Rosalie, and even though Lydia had never met her, she'd heard good things from some of her friends who'd gone to see her for various issues they were having in their lives. Lydia was a firm believer in getting help when help was needed—now, at least. Maybe if she and Luke had been more willing to open up about their problems all those years ago, they would never have been in this position.

Still, she thought as they approached the small two-story building where the therapist had her office, better late than never, right? Luke guided her up the narrow outdoor staircase to the office building's second story with a gentle hand on her back, and they both paused to take in the stunning panoramic ocean views when they reached the top.

"It's good to be back," Lydia murmured, resting her head on Luke's shoulder as she inhaled deeply, taking in as much of the fresh, salt-tinged air as she could. The island had been her home for most of her life, and she'd missed it terribly. Being able to spend time in Dolphin Bay again—and hopefully someday returning to the home she and Luke used to share—was a bonus of rekindling their relationship.

"It's good to have you back." Luke pressed his lips softly to her forehead, then let out a long sigh as they stared out over the rippling water. As they watched, the sun broke through a passing cloud, spreading its brilliant rays over the surface of the sea like shards of glittering glass. Below them, a lone woman walked along the sand, shoes in her hands, feet grazing the water. A dog bounded ahead of her, barking joyously as he danced in and out of the waves, tennis ball in his mouth.

"Are you ready for this?" Luke asked, his voice cutting into the silence that had settled between them.

Lydia nodded, feeling a ball of nerves forming in her stomach. "I am."

The door behind them opened just then and a middle-aged couple stepped out of the office, the woman holding a tissue to her nose, the man slightly red-faced. The ball in Lydia's gut solidified as she watched them walk away, their shoulders stiff and their gait awkward as they tried to avoid each other in the narrow walkway.

Luke's eyes were on them too, a nervous tic going in his jaw, and they both swung around in unison as a woman with auburn hair and a kind smile stepped out of the office and said, "Luke? Lydia? I'm Rosalie Barns. Please come in."

Lydia kept a tight grip on Luke's hand as they stepped into the office, which was small but decorated in soothing green tones. A large photo of a meadow hung on the wall, and beneath it was the chair that Rosalie settled into after gesturing for them to take the pair of comfortable-looking armchairs across from her. When everyone was seated, Rosalie set a notebook and pen on her lap, then folded her hands across them as she gave them both a kind smile.

Lydia returned a nervous one of her own; Luke looked rather pained.

"I understand your first session can be intimidating," Rosalie said, "but I want you to know that this office is a safe space for both of you to express your feelings without judgment. I'm going to let you guide our meeting today so I can get a sense of what's going on in your lives, what prompted you to decide to seek out a therapist." She smiled again. "There are a lot of misconceptions about going to therapy, one of them being that couples only attend when they're in crisis. That's absolutely not true—sometimes we just need some help communicating what we're thinking and feeling, and this is a place where we can work on that, as well as building on the foundation you already have. So." She crossed one leg over the other and relaxed into the chair, and Lydia could feel herself doing the same. "Where would you like to begin?"

Lydia slid a glance Luke's way—and saw that he was already watching her expectantly. The ball was in her court. "Well," she said, taking a deep breath, "I guess we're here because we're trying to rebuild our relationship. We were together for many years, married for some of them, but we divorced five years ago after..."

She hesitated, squeezing her eyes shut as the painful memories of the time before washed over her. Luke's grip on her hand grew tighter, more reassuring. When she opened her mouth to speak again, she found that she couldn't.

Luke released her hand and shifted his chair closer to hers so that they were practically touching, then linked her arm through his and gave her a reassuring smile as he leaned forward to speak, to fill in the blanks of the story that Lydia was still unable to tell.

"We tried for many years to have children, but we

weren't able to. There were many times when we had hope—" He stopped speaking abruptly, his voice catching. Then he shook his head and continued. "But each time ended in heartache. After a while, it began to wear on us. Our communication broke down to the point that we were barely speaking. We were each so lost in our grief that we weren't able to find each other. Then one day..."

He hesitated and glanced at Lydia. "One day, we decided we couldn't make things work anymore."

He was shielding her, protecting her, and Lydia knew it. But if they were going to truly find their way back to each other, they had to lay all their cards on the table, and be truthful about what had happened. About what she had done to him, to them. To herself.

"I walked out on him." Lydia's voice was small, barely above a whisper. "I couldn't take it anymore, and instead of trying one more time to work things out, I just... left."

"And how did that make you feel when it happened?" Rosalie turned her attention back to Luke.

Luke released a long breath, then unwound his arm from Lydia's—whether consciously or not, she couldn't tell. He gripped the arms of his chair, his knuckles slowly bleeding to white. "Hurt. Betrayed. Angry. Humiliated." He winced, then let his head fall back as he fixed his eyes on the ceiling. Lydia watched him, barely breathing; never before had she been forced to listen to the fallout of her actions from his point of view.

It was… awful.

Her eyes glistening with tears, she reached for him, but he kept his grip on the armrests. She let her hand fall back to her side and glanced at Rosalie, hoping the therapist hadn't noticed the slight. Her face remained neutral as she kept her attention focused on Luke, whose entire body was now tight with tension. "And how do you feel about it now?" she asked gently.

He was silent for a long moment, his eyes still on the ceiling. Then he slowly lowered his head until he was looking at Rosalie. "Hurt. Betrayed. Angry. Humiliated."

"I knew you blamed me." Ignoring the tears streaming down her cheeks, Lydia turned to him. "I knew you hated me."

"No." His eyes sought hers, and despite the deep hurt she saw in them, she saw something else, too.

Love.

"I've never hated you," he insisted. "Not then, not now. You weren't yourself, and I knew that. But that didn't make things any easier. In some ways, it made things worse—I couldn't put all the blame on your shoulders." He reached for her hand once more, and Lydia wiped at her eyes before turning to face Rosalie.

"I wanted so desperately to be a mother," she explained, needing to tell her side of the story. "Ever since I was a girl, I've been imagining it. The devastation I felt then—and that I still feel now—is something that I can't even begin to describe. It's with me, day in and day out. But despite what I've gone through, I know in my heart that someday I'll have a child. Someday I *will* be a mother." She had never voiced those thoughts out loud before, keeping them under lock and key in the deepest part of her soul, but once they were given life, she knew them to be true.

She immediately felt Luke stiffen beside her. "What?" he asked, turning to her with a look of disbelief. "You never said you still wanted to have children. How would you…?" His voice trailed off as he stared at her, and the look on his face could only be described as horrorstricken.

"There is more than one way to have a baby," Lydia said defensively, her eyes flicking to the therapist for support. The woman's face remained as neutral as ever as she watched the exchange. "I could try more fertility treatments, I could look into surrogacy, I could find an egg donor. Adoption is always an option, too."

By now, she could tell that her face was flushed with excitement; for the life of her, though, she couldn't understand why Luke didn't seem to share her feelings. Hadn't this been what they'd always wanted? They hadn't turned over every stone in their quest to have a child of their own; at the time Lydia had walked out that door, they were taking a break from the process, from the heartache, for a little while. It was Luke who had made the suggestion, with Lydia agreeing, albeit reluctantly.

When she reminded him of this, he looked floored. For several unending moments, he said nothing, merely rubbing one hand over his chin again and again as he stared at her like he'd never seen her before. Finally, when she could stand the silence no longer, he said, "We agreed to stop trying. Not just stop trying to have a baby the natural way—stop trying at all."

"No." Lydia shook her head so violently that her

hair whipped against her cheeks. "No, no, *no*. We agreed to stop trying *temporarily*. At least, that's what I agreed to. How could you think I would ever give up on becoming a mother?" She laughed harshly. "I would move mountains, Luke. I would literally move mountains."

"It was destroying us." Luke's voice was saturated with sorrow. "It *did* destroy us. I thought we had agreed to move forward together, just the two of us. Wasn't that what we were trying to do? Until you walked out." The last few words came out bitter. He stared hard at her, his gaze raking over her face before he met her eyes.

"Lydia." His voice was low, desperate. "I'm sorry. I can't go back to that—I won't. More fertility treatments, surrogates, egg donors, adoptions... it's making my head spin. No matter what you choose, it could lead to disappointment. It could lead to more heartbreak. Can you really recover from that again? Because I can't. I'm not willing to spend the next ten years of my life how we spent the past fifteen—miserable. It's time for me to move on."

"Never." Lydia could feel the tears streaming down her face. Rosalie passed her a tissue, and a startled Lydia accepted it—she'd forgotten the therapist was even in the room. "If you think I'd ever give up on becoming a mother, then I guess you don't know me as well as you think you do."

"No," Luke said, still looking stricken as he shook his head slowly, his eyes never leaving her face. "I guess I don't."

CHAPTER 11

Jax was in his element. The inn's expansive kitchen was filled with the mouth-watering scent of breakfast foods, and the sounds of cooking that had always put him at ease: eggs frying, pancakes sizzling, bread zipping in and out of the toaster. He had a spatula in one hand and a whisk in the other, eyes flicking between the griddle, where he was flipping a batch of blueberry pancakes, and the counter, where he was adding the ingredients for his vegetable omelets to a mixing bowl. Two pitchers of freshly squeezed juice were waiting on the counter opposite him—apple-blueberry and pineapple-orange, his personal favorite—and beside him, his niece Emery was busy spooning various flavors of jellies, jams, and butters into small ramekins.

"I don't know how you do it," she said, watching him with wide eyes as he flipped the last pancake onto a plate with one hand while simultaneously ladling eggs onto the griddle with the other. "I can't even do that trick where you rub your stomach with one hand and pat your head with the other." She set down the spoon she was holding and demonstrated; what started out as a rub-and-pat quickly devolved into random hand movements that had Jax chuckling in appreciation.

"I have plenty of practice," he said, sliding the plate of pancakes toward Emery, who immediately began arranging them on a polished silver serving tray that had probably been around since the inn's infancy. "I've worked in enough kitchens for pennies on the dollar to know my way around them."

"And now you're working in the big bad Inn at Dolphin Bay," Emery teased, pouring pure maple syrup that Tana had picked up at the local farmers' market into a tureen. After giving it a stir, she pushed aside the syrup and smiled at Jax. "We're really going to miss you around here, you know. The inn's not going to be the same without you." She gestured toward the griddle. "And neither is the breakfast. Have you found a replacement chef yet? My mom told me that Uncle Henry is leaving the hiring decisions up to you."

"Not yet," Jax said, wiping sweat from his brow with his sleeve before adding a generous heap of shredded cheese to the omelets and folding them over. "I put out a help wanted ad in a few local papers and job seeker websites, and I've gotten a few resumes over the past couple of days. I'm going to start taking a look at them once breakfast is over, actually." He grinned at her. "Unless you want me to train you for the job?"

"No thanks." Emery wrinkled her nose as she began arranging the ramekins of jellies and jams onto another serving tray and stacking piles of toast beside them. "I might be taking some time off to figure out what I want to do with my life, but living at the inn has shown me what I *don't* want to do... and that's running an inn. Unlike my mother." She gave Jax a sad smile. "She won't admit how heart-broken she is that she's not needed around here as much."

"Running an inn, especially one like this that has been in a family for generations, is a labor of love, and Tana loves this place." He swept his arms around the kitchen. "But it's also much more than a full-time job—it's a way of life. Mornings, nights, holidays, weekends—you have to be available for all of it. Between you and me, even though Uncle Henry is making incredible strides in his recovery, I can't imagine he'll be able to run the inn for much longer." He laughed as he pictured the old man's ornery face. "But no one can tell him that—it's a conclusion he'll have to reach on his own."

"And he'll never reach it." Emery shook her head, her long dark hair falling over her shoulders. "But Mom's in such a tizzy over what she's going to do next—I think when she came here, she didn't realize her temporary move was going to become so permanent. She left California without needing to think about the future, and now that she does, she's panicking." She shrugged. "I'm not sure what all the fuss is about, honestly. It's not like Uncle Henry's going to kick her out to the curb."

Jax gave his niece a gentle smile; she wasn't old enough to understand yet that life—and especially the unknowns of life—could be frightening, setting you adrift in a stormy sea without a lifeboat. "I'm sure everything will work out just fine," he said. "I offered her a place with me in Miami Beach," he added in a playful tone, "but something tells me she's not going to take me up on it."

"No way Mom's leaving the island, especially now that she's met Reed." Emery watched as Jax put the finishing touches on the omelets, and then slid them onto yet another platter.

Today's guests at the inn were going to be treated to a breakfast fit for an army of hungry teenagers, Jax thought, surveying the offerings. He suspected he'd gotten a bit carried away—something he tended to do in the kitchen when his mind was wandering and his body was tense with anxiety. Cooking had always been a balm to his nerves, and now that the conversation had taken a turn to his upcoming cross-country move, he had the urge to slap a few dozen more sausages on the griddle.

His niece hadn't noticed anything was amiss, though, and she continued chatting away as she grabbed handfuls of silverware from the drawers and stuffed them into holders. "If you want company, though, *I* would always be happy to take you up on a trip to Miami. That place must be paradise."

"Dolphin Bay is paradise." Jax said the words without thinking, but once they were out of his mouth, he knew them to be true. "Miami Beach is great, don't get me wrong," he added hastily when Emery raised her eyebrows and regarded him curiously. "It's got plenty to offer, especially if you like flash and excitement. But…" He let his voice drift off, the rest of his sentence hovering in the air between them.

Emery cocked her head to one side, her eyes narrowing as she studied his face. "Uncle Jax, are you having second thoughts?"

"No," he said, more forcefully than he'd intended. Her eyebrows rose another notch, her look of disbelief intensifying. "No," he repeated, more firmly this time, suggesting that the conversation was closed.

His niece, however, didn't take the hint. "I think you are. And I think I know why." Her lips curved in a sly smile that had Jax staring at her in bewilderment.

"Why?"

The kitchen door swung open, and both of them turned to see Uncle Henry standing in the doorway. "Everyone's seated," he said, his eyes sweeping over the assortment of breakfast foods now lined up on the counter. He gave Jax an approving nod. "Looks good. We'll miss you around here." Beckoning to Emery, he added, "Let's start bringing out the drinks."

Jax, grateful for the abrupt end to what was quickly becoming an uncomfortable conversation, turned back to the griddle. He slid the last few slices of crisp bacon onto a tray, set it alongside the others, and untied his apron with a sigh. Emery gave him a look that plainly said *This conversation isn't over* before grabbing the pitchers of juice and following Henry out of the kitchen.

After washing and toweling off his hands, Jax sank onto the nearest stool and slid his phone out of his pocket, pulling up the Internet tabs he'd been perusing that morning. His move was marching steadily closer, and for some reason, he'd been unable to bring himself to search for apartments; when he woke up this morning and forced himself to look at the calendar, he realized that he couldn't put off the task a minute longer.

Page after page of rental listings stared back at him: sleek oceanside condos, Spanish-style bungalows, cozy houses surrounded by Florida's lush and colorful plant life. Emery was right: it truly was a paradise. Then Jax wandered to the kitchen's window, smaller than the huge picture windows in the parlor and dining room but with a breathtaking view all the same: the cerulean ocean, rippling gently in the saltwater breeze; the knee-length dune grass swaying in the wind, brushing against the worn dirt path that led to the golden sand; the endless sky above the island's shimmering coastline.

There was no greater paradise than Dolphin Bay.

He didn't appreciate it when he was a kid, angry at first for being dumped here each summer but growing to long for the days when he, Tana, and Daphne would run wild on the island's streets, the beach their playground. Melting ice cream cones, legs stretched over the boardwalk, feet threatening to lose the tenuous grip on their sandals over the churning water. Laughter—the girls' high-pitched and giggling, his lower, deeper, devil-may-care. Stolen looks and shy smiles. Hidden kisses and the ache of first love. He had experienced all of it on the island.

When he said goodbye the last time, he vowed never to return. Now, he hadn't even left yet, and he couldn't wait to come back.

To come home.

And what did home mean to him, truly? Not the childhood one he shared with his mother, that much was for certain. Not even the inn.

Home meant sunshine-colored hair and a freckled nose. It meant a girl with awkward angles and gangly limbs who had grown into the kind of woman who made men stop in their tracks to turn and stare. Home meant a soft laugh and softer hands. It meant sun-kissed skin and salty lips.

When he thought of that word, he could only picture one face.

The girl who had stolen his heart long ago, and the woman who continued to hold it captive.

DAPHNE HUMMED to herself as she spun the three-tiered cake on its platform, smoothing down the lines and notches in the buttercream. She finally had a break from the bakery's early morning rush, with several of her fellow islanders waiting outside the shop as she unlocked the doors, eager to scoop up their pick of the fresh donuts. Now only a middle-aged couple she didn't recognize remained in the bakery, quietly talking as they enjoyed their muffins and coffee—a recent addition, thanks to Jax's skill in setting up the newfangled espresso and latte machine she'd purchased.

Now that she had a few minutes to catch her breath, she was focusing on the next challenge she planned to tackle: wedding cakes, beginning with the one she had designed for Edie and Henry. As Edie requested, and to Daphne's relief, the cake was simple yet elegant, with ivory buttercream frosting, a delicate pearl design, and tasteful piping around the edges. The top and sides would be adorned with coral roses, and the cake batter was a to-die-for almond with fresh raspberry filling.

The wedding was quickly approaching, and Daphne had spent enough time practicing that she felt reasonably confident she wouldn't deliver them a mess on their big day… although the waistband of her jeans had started to become uncomfortably tight, courtesy of the many practice tiers she'd stashed in the freezer.

"That was delicious, thank you," a woman said behind her, and Daphne turned from the counter to find that the couple had finished their muffins and drained the last of their coffee. As the woman waited for her husband to stash their muffin wrappers and cups in the trash can, she leaned on the bakery's display case to make small talk with Daphne. "This is our first time in Dolphin Bay, and between this bakery and the inn we're staying at, I'm not sure we're ever going to leave."

Daphne smiled at her, knowing she could only be referring to one place. "The Inn at Dolphin Bay? It's an island institution, and it's recently undergone an amazing set of renovations."

"Well whatever they've done, it's absolutely stunning." The man approached the counter and put his arm around his wife. "Are you ready to head to the beach? I can't remember the last time I've seen such a glorious day."

She patted her husband's stomach and laughed. "You're on a sugar rush. And speaking of that, I think we'll take a few treats with us for the road."

As she perused the cupcakes and slices of cake that Daphne had set out that morning, the bell above the door chimed and in walked Jax. Daphne held up a finger, indicating that he should wait, and he nodded and slipped into an empty table by the window, resting his fist under his chin as he gazed out at the passersby strolling along the town's main square.

Daphne watched him for a moment, an undeniable feeling of regret washing over her, but did her best to return her attention to the couple, who were now arguing good-naturedly over which flavors of cupcake they wanted.

After boxing up their treats and waving them out the door, Daphne stepped out from behind the counter, tugging her ponytail tighter and brushing some of the flour from her buttercream-smeared apron. "To what do I owe the honor?" she asked as she slid into the seat across from him. Outside, a single seagull soared through the air, its gray wingtips shimmering in the morning sunshine. They both watched it until it disappeared from sight, gliding over the water before dipping into the waves, presumably to find its morning meal.

Jax retrieved his phone from his pocket and set it on the table between them, flicking his finger up the screen to reveal a website with several photos of a property with majestic ocean views. "What's all this?" she asked, sliding it closer so she could study the photos. The property looked to be on one of the top floors of a tall condo building, with a pristine pool, white marble floors, and tall palm trees lining the walkway that led directly onto the sand.

"This is Miami. Beautiful, isn't it?" He studied her face, as if expecting some sort of reaction.

Daphne merely graced him with a noncommittal shrug. "Sure, if you like glitz and glamor. You're really going to be able to afford a place like that?"

"Maybe someday." He gave her his trademark mischievous grin. "If I can, will you come and visit me?"

She shifted uncomfortably on the chair as her eyes wandered to the bakery's door, but no customers—or interruptions—were in sight. "I'm sure Tana and I will manage a trip down there at some point. After all the stress of opening the bakery, a girls' trip will be in order. Someday, if I can get away for a few days." She laughed, but Jax didn't join in.

Instead, he folded his hands on the table and looked at her, his eyes searching hers. "Daphne, do you want me to go?"

She looked away. "I want you to do whatever makes you happy."

His gaze was unflinching. "But do you *want* me to go? Do you want me to leave the island?" All traces of humor were gone from his face.

"I..." Daphne hesitated, flustered, unsure where this conversation was headed. Finally, she reached across the table and rested her hand on his. "Jax, this is an amazing opportunity, and I'm happy for you. We all want the best for you, me included. Besides," she added, careful to keep her tone light, "this isn't goodbye forever. Tana is here, and Henry... you'll be back to visit."

Jax exhaled softly as he stared down at their hands, still touching. When he met her gaze again, sadness was heavy in his eyes. "Let me ask this a different way. Do you want me to stay?"

"No. Yes. I don't know." Daphne withdrew her

hand and rested it on her lap, curling it into a fist. "Whatever makes you happy, Jax. And I don't think that's being here, on the island. So I guess what I'm saying is… no. I don't want you to stay."

Jax was quiet for a long moment after that, his gaze wandering back out to the window. The couple who had just been in the bakery emerged from an adjacent souvenir store with shopping bags, giving Daphne a cheerful wave as they walked by, headed toward the beach. Jax watched them until they rounded the corner, and when he turned back to her, his face was blank.

"Okay then." He braced his hands against the edge of the table and rose. "That's all I needed to know."

And then he walked out the door without another word, leaving her to stare after him long after he'd disappeared from view.

CHAPTER 12

"Here's to my mother." Laurie held her champagne glass high in the air as she grinned down at Edie. "The most wonderful woman I've ever known, and my role model in every way. I know I speak for everyone in this room when I wish you and Henry a beautiful wedding day, and a long and happy life together. We love you more than words."

Edie smiled at her daughter as the assembled guests clapped and raised their own glasses in a toast. Then she turned to Henry and squeezed his hand tightly, mouthing the words *I love you*. As his green eyes met hers, she saw in them a blend of love and disbelief, a feeling she shared. Edie looked around the room, suppressing the urge to pinch herself to make sure she wasn't dreaming.

In truth, she never thought they'd be here. It had taken twenty years of friendship that had slowly morphed into something more before Henry was willing to admit the depths of his feelings for her. But now, here they were, on the eve of their wedding, enjoying a celebratory dinner with all the people they loved. Edie's children and grandchildren were here, as were Tana and Emery, Daphne, and several of Edie's closest friends.

They'd chosen to keep tonight's festivities intimate; tomorrow, nearly all of the island's residents would be joining them on the beach as they vowed to spend the rest of their lives together. Henry had initially wanted the wedding to be a quiet affair as well, but word about the couple's engagement had spread around Dolphin Bay like wildfire, and Edie found herself inviting more and more friends and neighbors to join them in their joy until she took a step back and realized she'd invited half the town.

So why not invite the other half too? Edie had always liked to throw a party, and oh, what a party this was going to be. Henry, bless his heart, had gone along with her wishes, but she knew he was more than a little anxious about being the center of all that attention.

Edie's eyes lingered on the beloved faces around the table, stopping when she caught sight of Reed, her beautiful boy, with his arm tucked snugly around Tana's waist. If she were a betting woman, she would place good odds that the two of them would be next down the aisle. At least she very much hoped so; she had never seen her son happier than he had been these past few months, and she couldn't have hand-picked anyone better than Tana.

"I guess it's my turn." Karina gave the table a nervous smile as she pushed back her chair and reached for her champagne glass, and Edie immediately turned her attention to her elder daughter. "Mom, Henry, I'll be honest: when I first heard about your relationship, I was a little hesitant."

She turned to Henry, her eyes warm. "I didn't think there was a man on this earth who deserved my mother, but I was wrong. Over the past few months, I've watched her blossom. I've watched her laugh like a teenager again. I've watched her act like a woman in love. You have treated her with the kind of respect and kindness that a daughter could only dream of for her mother, and for that, I thank you, from the bottom of my heart. She deserves the best, and you have proven yourself to be just that." She raised her glass in a toast, and Edie took a moment to pat her eyes dry before joining in.

When Karina rounded the table toward her, Edie stood, preparing to give her daughter a hug—but she wasn't heading for Edie. Instead, she bent down and wrapped her arms around Henry's neck, whispering something in his ear that Edie wasn't privy to. When she pulled away, Henry gave her a gentle smile and murmured, "It's my honor to." Karina gripped his shoulder, then turned to give her mother a kiss on the cheek before returning to her seat.

Reed stood next, clearing his throat and smiling at his mother and Henry in turn. "My sisters said everything so eloquently that I'm not sure what's left for me. That's what happens when you're the only boy and the youngest in the family—you always get squashed under their shoes."

He made to sit down, and those in the room chuckled appreciatively. Then he straightened up, one hand in the pocket of his suit coat, the other lightly holding his champagne glass. "I've been my mother's right-hand man for the past twenty years, and I've enjoyed every second of it. Without her, I would never have moved to the island, I would never have started my own business, and I would never have met the stunningly beautiful woman sitting next to me tonight."

Tana lowered her gaze to the table in embarrassment, but Edie could see that her cheeks were pink with pleasure. "Tomorrow, I'm going to pass that responsibility to someone else," Reed continued, turning to face Henry. "And I couldn't have chosen a better man for the job than you. You make my mother happy. To me, that's always been enough."

He raised his glass higher in the air. "To the beautiful couple. May you have many years of love, friendship, and every good thing that life has to offer. I love you both."

After another round of glass-clinking, Edie drained the last of her champagne and leaned into Henry, who wrapped his arm around her waist and held her close to him. "Are you ready for tomorrow?" he whispered as the string quartet they'd hired for the evening picked up their instruments and began to play a romantic melody.

"I am." Edie stroked her fingers down his cheek. "I've been waiting for this moment for years, Henry. Nothing could stop me from walking down that aisle." She paused and tapped a finger to her chin. "Well, I guess I don't mean that." When he looked at her in alarm, she said, "If you show up in slippers,

I'm going to have Reed toss you right into the ocean."

Henry chuckled, soft and low, and gathered her in his arms once more; they bent their heads together and listened to the soft music floating up toward the restaurant's rafters.

The rest of the evening passed far too quickly for Edie's liking, and she soon found herself back in her own house, listening to her daughters talking quietly in the next room; as her matrons of honor, they would be spending the night with her, and would wake up early to begin the wedding preparations. Normally she would be glad for the company—she'd spent far too many nights puttering around this house by herself—but once they'd returned from dinner, a feeling of melancholy swept over her unexpectedly. Before her daughters noticed her change in mood, she'd given several exaggerated yawns and proclaimed that she needed all the beauty sleep she could get, but she knew that tonight, sleep would be elusive.

Instead, she was sitting on her bed, a photo album in her lap, tracing her fingers along the worn white cover, which was embossed with the date of what had been—and still remained—the most important day of her life. It was hard to believe that more than two decades had passed since she'd last seen Johnny's face, or heard his voice, or held his hand in hers. He had been her first love, her everything, and to have him taken from her at such a young age was cruel, and brutal, and something no woman should ever have to endure. Watching her beloved husband waste away for months had been pain beyond anything she could imagine, and when he finally found peace, she vowed she would never put herself through anything like that again.

But tomorrow, she would do just that. Marrying Henry would leave her vulnerable once more; this time, even more so. As a young bride, her face alight with happiness as she clung to Johnny's arm, Edie had never given a second thought to what would happen when one of them was no longer there, when the life they were planning would come to an end. It seemed unfathomable, when they were dewy with youth and radiant with love and happiness.

Now, she knew better. There would come a day, perhaps in the not so distant future, when either her or Henry would have to say goodbye for a final time, when the light in their eyes would dim, when the love they shared would be a memory tucked away in the heart of the one left behind.

This time, though, she was lucky. She knew to

live each day together as though it would be the last, to savor the routines, the mundane conversations, the unremarkable habits of everyday life. She'd learned long ago that those were the things that would be remembered, when all of it came to an end. Because in truth, Edie could barely remember her and Johnny's wedding day; but she would never forget the absentminded kiss on the lips he gave her every morning on his way out the door, briefcase in hand. She couldn't remember all the details of the fancy anniversary dinners they'd shared, but she would never, *ever,* forget the feel of his hand in hers.

Most people were lucky to find love once in their life. Edie was blessed to find it twice. And this time, she was going to savor every moment of it.

She glanced at the clock; it was nearing midnight, and she and her daughters planned to be up at the crack of dawn to enjoy breakfast together before the start of the festivities.

Time to say goodnight.

"I adore you, Johnny," she said, trailing her finger along his face, laughing and handsome, the boy who'd swept her off her feet and taught her what it was like to love unconditionally. To still love unconditionally, even after all these years. "And I always will."

Bending down, she pressed a gentle kiss to the photograph, then let her eyes linger on his face for a few moments longer before she quietly closed the album and turned off the light.

TANA YAWNED WIDELY, then glanced around the airport in embarrassment, hoping no one had seen her. The baggage claim area was nearly empty at this hour; other than herself, there was a man seated in the far corner, his head lolling against the wall beside him as he drifted in and out of sleep, and a private driver holding a sign with his passenger's last name.

Why did her mother decide to take such a late flight, anyway? Edie and Henry had planned an early-afternoon wedding, so by the time Tana returned to the inn, Julie in tow, she'd barely be able to catch a few hours of sleep before she needed to help with the wedding preparations.

A speaker somewhere in the airport's ceiling crackled to life, and a bored male voice announced an incoming flight number that Tana couldn't even begin to make out. She made her way over to the flight tracker, noting, with a thankful sigh, that her mother's plane had just landed. Still, Tana couldn't suppress the nagging feeling in the pit of her stomach that her mother wouldn't actually be *on* that plane. Julie was like dandelion puff blowing in the wind—you never knew where she was going to land, and most of the time, neither, it seemed, did she.

But the look in Uncle Henry's eyes when Tana told him that Julie would be attending the wedding wasn't one she'd soon forget, and she hoped, for his sake, that her mother considered those around her for a change. Jax had flat-out refused to accompany Tana to the airport, so she was here to greet their mother, and escort her back to the inn, alone.

The clock on the airport's wall seemed to be moving in slow motion as Tana watched the numbers tick forward, until she finally heard a commotion above her as the tram doors opened and the flight's passengers began streaming down the stairs and escalator toward baggage claim. Suddenly alert, Tana searched the sea of faces for her mother, her nerves ratcheting up higher and higher as each person who was decidedly not Julie Keller strode past. When the last passenger, a gray-haired man barking orders into his cell phone, pushed past her on his way to the driver still holding the name card, Tana's heart dropped into her feet.

She wasn't coming. She really wasn't coming.

Jax would be thrilled, at least. Uncle Henry? Tana couldn't even bear the thought of breaking the news to him, especially on the morning of his wedding.

Tana had just turned to leave when she caught movement out of the corner of her eye, and swung back around to see the tram doors opening and her mother stepping out. She was wearing her usual photography uniform: man's button-down shirt, the sleeves rolled up past her elbows; baggy cargo pants; and a kerchief around her neck, this one safari-themed. Her gray-blonde hair hung past her shoulders, and slung across her chest was her camera equipment. She scanned the empty airport, her eyes immediately landing on Tana.

"Hello*o*!" she called, waving one arm enthusiastically as she used the other to wheel her suitcase to the escalator. After she descended, she released the handle of her suitcase, letting it fall to the floor with a clatter, and flung her arms around Tana's neck. "Oh, honey girl, I can't tell you how good it is to see you!"

Tana tried not to tense in her mother's arms, or cringe at the use of the girlhood nickname, instead allowing her mother to step back and look her up and down. "My, aren't you a sight for sore eyes. You look beautiful—I guess divorce has really done wonders for you, hasn't it?"

"Technically I'm not—" Tana began, but her mother continued speaking as though she hadn't heard her.

"Last time I saw you, you looked frumpy-dumpy, but now?" She whistled. "Let me guess: someone's got a new man in her life." Julie was speaking loud enough that two men passing by smirked at Tana, who closed her eyes briefly, wishing she could disappear through the floor.

"Thanks," she said, gritting her teeth against the backhanded compliment. "You look well too. Are you ready to go? We need to make it to the harbor in time to catch the last ferry, and"—she groaned, catching sight of her watch—"we're already running fifteen minutes late."

"Sorry about that," Julie said, falling into step beside her daughter. "I spent the whole flight thinking about a series of shots I took of the desert tortoise in Zion National Park, and when I got off the plane, I just had to pull out my computer and check the angle to make sure I captured the pattern on their shells correctly. You know how it is when—"

Tana found herself drifting into her own

thoughts as her mother began waxing poetic about the finer points of wildlife photography, something that Tana not only had zero interest in, but actively despised—in large part, she was sure, because even as a child she knew that Julie loved the animals she stalked with a lens far more than her own children.

The cab ride to the ferry was much the same, with Tana nodding or grunting once in a while in response to her mother's steady stream of words; only when she tried to bring up Derek's engagement did Tana come to, tearing her eyes away from the scenery outside the cab's back window to say sharply, "You know what? I'd rather not talk about that."

Especially with you, she wanted to add, but kept silent. Not once since Tana's separation had her mother called to check on her; in fact, the only time she'd heard from her in months was when she called to ask Tana to care for Uncle Henry in her place. Fortunately, Tana had agreed—she shuddered to think what her life would be like now if she hadn't. So in a way, Tana supposed she should thank Julie for her selfishness.

They caught the ferry just in time, and Tana spent the trip to the island lost in thought, imagining all the ways her life had changed since she'd stepped foot in Dolphin Bay for the first time since she was a teenager, while her mother dozed in the row of seats across from her, exhausted from the long trip. When the ferry glided into the harbor, she jolted awake, staring around in confusion as she brushed her hair out of her eyes before her gaze landed on Tana—and behind her, the island in all its nighttime glory.

"It's good to be back," Julie murmured as she followed Tana down the ramp, falling into step beside her as their feet hit the boardwalk's weathered wooden planks. Tana felt herself relaxing as they threaded their way up the path that led to the main part of town, glad to be home at last. She glanced into the distance, in the direction of Reed's home, and felt a sudden strong tug in her heart, a need to see him, to hold him, to thank him for all he had become to her these past few months.

"Definitely a new man," her mother said in a sly voice, continuing their conversation from the airport as she caught sight of the tender smile on Tana's lips. "I recognize that look anywhere. Is he good to you?"

"The best." Tana met her mother's eyes. "He's the absolute best."

"Good." Julie gave a brisk nod. "Then I'm looking

forward to meeting him. You needed a man to pick you up off the ground. No thanks to Derek."

Tana felt herself bristling. "I don't *need* anyone," she said, stopping in her tracks to turn and face her mother. "I met him, and we became friends, and we fell in love. He's a partner to me; he's not my knight in shining armor. I don't need that from him, and I never have."

Julie made a noncommittal sound that set Tana's teeth on edge, somewhere between a *hmm* and a snort.

"What?" Tana demanded. "Just say whatever it is you're thinking—you always do anyway."

Instead of reacting with anger, Julie gave her daughter a serene smile. "I don't mean to *insult* you, honey girl. What I mean is…" She sighed, then screwed up her mouth in thought. "Since you were a little girl, you would cling to whoever was around you—me, Jax, your grandparents when you used to stay with them. You were never independent. You were never like me, a go-getter, a woman with a vision for herself and a career. You were always a little… soft. Delicate, I should say." She shrugged. "There's nothing wrong with that." But her tone of voice said otherwise.

Tana stared hard at the woman who raised her—

or, in this case, didn't. "I was a good wife to Derek, and a wonderful mother to Emery. I pride myself on those things. If you want to take that away from me, that's on you. I know the truth." She took a deep breath, trying to rein in her anger. No good could come of trying to argue her perspective with Julie; she'd learned that long ago.

Her mother gave her another sly look. "Maybe you do have some fire in you after all." By now they had reached the inn, and Tana used her key to unlock the door and slip into the dim foyer. The guests were in bed for the night, as was Henry; only Jax's light still glowed from beneath his closed bedroom door.

"Oh, it's good to be back," Julie said softly as she glanced around the inn. "And it looks just beautiful —I see Uncle Henry's doing as well as ever."

This time, it was Tana's turn to grunt a response. Her mother had failed to check in on Henry, too, in the aftermath of his stroke, and as such, had no idea the state of disrepair the inn had been in when Tana first walked through the door. All the months of planning, of worrying, of working late into the night and rising before dawn to do it all over again—Julie was privy to none of it.

And right now, Tana wouldn't have it any other way.

"Where's Jax?" Julie looked at the front desk, as if expecting to see him behind the computer. "I hope he's able to make it too. Of course, he's a busy man—it takes a lot to run your own restaurant. Tell me, was he able to fly in from Philadelphia?"

Tana's eyes lingered on her mother's face for a long moment while she debated how to respond. Finally, she smiled and said, "Yes, he was. But he's sleeping now, so you won't be able to see him until tomorrow."

Dropping her purse on the floor and kicking off her shoes with a sigh, she motioned toward her mother and then grabbed her suitcase. "Now come with me, and I'll show you to your room."

CHAPTER 13

"Here I am, ready, willing, and at your service."

Luke's grin was impossibly wide as Tana opened the inn's front door and peered at him through bleary eyes. It was just past dawn, and she'd spent much of the night tossing and turning, working her half-awake self into a frenzy at the thought of all that could go wrong in the lead-up to the wedding.

The minister could come down with a bad case of the stomach flu. A seagull could swoop down and gobble up half the cake. The sky could open up and send sheets of rain onto the bride, groom, and unsuspecting guests. They could all get food poisoning from the clam chowder that Uncle Henry had insisted on adding to the menu. And on and on it went, all night long, a merry-go-round of tragedies, until her head was pounding and her stomach was roiling.

"You're way too chipper," she said, covering up a massive yawn with one hand as she turned and padded back into the inn, Luke at her heels. Then, seeing that no one had entered behind him, she frowned, standing on tiptoes to see into the inn's parking lot. Empty.

"Where's Lydia?" she asked, feeling slightly panicked. Luke's former wife—and current girlfriend—was a popular wedding planner, and Tana had relied on her expertise several times over the past few weeks as the wedding preparations marched steadily forward. "I thought she said she was coming to help out today."

Luke's smile fell. "Sorry about that—there was an emergency back home, something with her mother, I don't know all the details. She asked me to send you her apologies, and her well wishes for the happy couple." His eyes skirted away from hers for a brief moment before the grin returned and he spread his arms wide. "But she sent her best assistant in her place—like I said, I'm all yours for the day."

Tana decided not to press the matter; it was obvious from the scant details and Luke's nonchalant attitude that he wasn't telling her something, but now was not the time for mysteries. It was the time for panic, she thought, catching sight of the sky for the first time and noting, with horror, the gray clouds looming overhead. For the umpteenth time over the past few weeks, she silently cursed the happy couple for inviting the entire island to their celebration; what had started out as plans for an intimate family affair had quickly ballooned to a three-hundred-person party. Also for the umpteenth time over the past few weeks, she regretted volunteering to oversee the entire event.

Along with Emery, Jax, and, apparently, Luke. A motley crew if one had ever existed, but right now, Tana would take what she could get.

And speaking of which…

She glanced at the clock, and then up to the inn's second floor, where Jax's and Emery's bedroom doors were still closed, the lights off.

This wouldn't do. This wouldn't do at all.

"THERE WAS one New Year's Eve at my restaurant where I worked from nine o'clock in the morning until three a.m. the following day, and I'll tell you, that was *nothing* compared to this." Jax was slumped in one of the white Chiavari chairs set up in rows along the sand, his forehead streaming with sweat. Emery was lying across three chairs in the row behind him, fanning her face and neck with one of the ceremony programs, her long hair drifting into the sand. Luke was chugging from a bottle of water, his face red, the back of his shirt streaked with sweat as he straddled a chair beside her.

Tana alone was still standing, hands on hips as she surveyed their handiwork. Over the past few hours, they had singlehandedly set up more than three hundred chairs, tying red satin bows over the back of each one; erected the canopy where Edie and Henry would say their vows and draped its top and sides with filmy white fabric that was now blowing softly in the ocean breeze; unfurled the aisle runner; scattered rose petals all over the sand; and set up stations for drinks so the guests could stay cool. And all of that under a blistering and unforgiving sun whose gift to the happy couple was an unseasonably hot day. But at least the threat of rain seemed to have passed, Tana thought as she shot a grateful glance up at the sky, clear and blue except for a few puffy clouds drifting by.

"Don't get too comfortable," she warned her

helpers. "We still have to set up the tables, chairs, decorations, and dance floor for the cocktail hour and reception." Just the thought of all that work made Tana's head swim, but Henry and Edie were on a limited budget; if Tana and the gang didn't help out, who would? At the end of the day, she was happy to—especially if it freed the couple from stress and allowed them to enjoy their wedding to the fullest.

Besides, all this hard work would make dinner, drinks, and dancing tonight seem all the more sweet. She was excited for the festivities, and had gone shopping with Emery to choose a new dress for the occasion. The figure-hugging emerald-green dress with a slit up the leg and an off-the-shoulder neckline was a far cry from the black gowns she usually chose to wear, but her daughter assured her that she would have Reed's head spinning around in a full circle when he saw her for the first time.

"There's that smile again," Emery said playfully, raising herself up on her elbows and nodding toward Tana, who quickly tried to cover it. "I've been on the island long enough now to recognize it —she's thinking about Reed." Her daughter's eyes twinkled as she nudged Jax in the side. "Aren't they just the cutest couple you've ever seen? Outside of Edie and Uncle Henry, that is."

"They're just darling," Jax said with a groan as he dragged himself off the chair and shot an envious look at Luke's empty water bottle. "Thanks for sharing, by the way."

"Sorry." Luke glanced around in vain for another drink, then gestured toward the ocean. "God's water fountain. Might be a bit salty, though."

"You should see Mom's dress," Emery continued, rising to her feet and gathering up the remaining chair ribbons. "She looks hot. I bet Reed won't be able to keep his hands off her."

"Please." Jax held up a hand with a wince. "Spare me, okay? I've got enough to worry about right now without having to think about someone pawing at my sister."

"You know who else I bet is going to look beautiful?" Emery continued blithely, as if her uncle hadn't been talking. "Daphne." She shot him a knowing look. "I wonder if she's bringing a date tonight?"

Jax mumbled something incoherent, and then, looking bad-tempered, he began trudging through the sand toward the tents that would soon become the location of dinner and dancing under the stars. Tana watched him go, her lips twitching with amusement as she shook her head and wondered why love always had to be so complicated.

"OH, Mom. I—I don't even know what to say." Karina pressed her fingers to her lips as her eyes welled up with tears. "There's never been a more beautiful bride."

"If you think that now, you should have seen me when I was twenty-four," Edie teased as she studied her reflection in the full-length mirror. The ivory gown was just as perfect now as the day she chose it, with its stunning lace design and simple silhouette that softened her curves in all the right places.

She smiled at herself in the mirror, allowing the years to drip away, seeing not the gray-haired woman she was now but the girl who had come before, blonde and dewy-skinned and ready to take on the world. Then she pulled herself back to the present, taking a moment to admire the woman who stood before her now: older, wiser, but no less young at heart. And ready to take on the world—a new world—just the same.

Lifting her gown off the floor, she padded over to her jewelry box and selected a pair of diamond earrings that Johnny had given her for a wedding gift, knowing he would approve of her using them today. He had always wanted her to be happy, to move on with her life; from the time he'd found out he was sick, he'd been adamant about it. Knowing that brought her a sense of peace—and wearing those earrings allowed him to be part of this moment, a song in her heart she would always carry with her.

Her daughters' tears flowed freely as she slid on the earrings, and when she turned and opened her arms to them, the three women hugged each other tightly until a knock on the door interrupted them. They released each other, and Laurie turned to open it, revealing a grinning Reed standing in the doorway.

"Is this still a girls-only club, or am I allowed in?" And then he caught sight of his mother, and his face softened.

"Mom, you look beautiful." He kissed her gently on the cheek, and when he pulled away, his eyes were shining. "What a lucky guy I am to get to walk you down the aisle. And speaking of which." He tapped his watch. "Are you ready to get married?"

"Almost." Edie reached out and straightened the lapels of her son's gray suit, admiring how handsome he looked. These days, she was used to seeing him in casual beach clothes—jeans and a T-shirt were staples of his wardrobe—but today, he took her breath away. As did her daughters, both of them lovely in the long pink dresses they'd chosen together, their dark hair swept up in elegant chignons. She beckoned her children closer until they were standing in a circle, clasping hands, holding on tight.

"I want to thank you for all that you've done for me over the past twenty years since we lost your father," she whispered, a lone tear trickling down her face as her eyes lingered on their beloved faces. "Without your support, and your unconditional love, I never would have survived. I never would have been standing here today, happier than I thought was possible."

She smiled at each of them in turn. "You've opened your hearts to Henry, and words can't describe how much that means to me. To have the three of you standing by my side today is a blessing and an honor, and I want you to know that I love you—forever, for always, no matter what." She whispered those last words, the ones she always ended each day with when her children were young, the words they carried with them to sleep.

For a few moments after that, there was nothing but the sound of quiet sniffles as her children reached for tissues. She dabbed her own eyes, then turned toward the mirror, smoothing down her dress before gently lifting the bouquet of coral roses from her bedside table. After a deep breath and a quiet prayer for a joyful future, she grinned and said, "Now who's ready to party?"

CHAPTER 14

"Uncle Henry?" Tana called as she knocked twice on the bedroom door. "Are you ready? Everything's all set. Jax is just heading outside to grab the golf cart—he's going to drive you down to the beach, and the rest of us will meet you there."

"Give me just a minute." Henry kept his eyes fixed on the view outside his window—it was a glorious day on the island, the crisp sky above the swirling blues and greens of the ocean almost too perfect to be believable. He hadn't expected this; had, in fact, expected a monsoon, or a tornado, or an earthquake, or some other act of God that would prevent the day from ever happening. So, for the past two hours, he'd been sitting in his chair by the window, eyes glued to the outside world, stomach churning with nerves.

But the sun continued to cast its rays over the sparkling water just the same, and somewhere on this island, the woman he loved was preparing to walk down the aisle to him, and him alone.

It was almost too unbelievable to be believable at all.

Did that make sense? Henry wasn't sure. Nor did he care—it made sense to him.

He was eighty-three years old. A lifelong bachelor. A loner. A hermit—according to his neighbors, he suspected. He wasn't supposed to be getting married. And especially not to Edie Dawes, the most beautiful, vivacious, kind-hearted woman he'd ever had the pleasure of knowing. Every so often, as he sat in that chair, waiting for the sky to fall, he pinched himself, just to make sure the past few months hadn't been a dream.

It hurt every time.

Just last year, the idea of him sharing his life with someone would have been preposterous. How much had changed since then. And how much would continue to change. For the first time since his mother passed away, too many years ago to count, someone else besides him would be calling the inn home. Edie had already begun moving her belongings into his bedroom, the lotions and potions and womanly things that were completely out of place but perfect all the same. She would keep her house too; Henry had grudgingly agreed to spend some of his time there as well, when Tana was caring for the inn in his place.

So much change, for a man who had changed so little over the years. In the past, the idea of starting a new life would have been terrifying. Now, he welcomed it with open arms.

He glanced at his cane leaning against the nightstand, then rose from the chair, bracing his hand against the windowsill for support. After taking a moment to gather his balance, he made his way over to the mirror, re-straightening his bow tie and patting down a single strand of hair that had fallen out of place. He couldn't remember the last time he'd worn a suit. He'd never had occasion to. The man staring back at him was almost unrecognizable—not because of the suit he wore but because of the new light in his eyes.

The hope. The excitement. The promise of a future he had always secretly dreamed of.

"Uncle Henry?" Tana knocked again, her voice

hesitant. "We really should be going. You don't want to be late."

No. He didn't.

He'd waited long enough.

"WHERE'S MOM?" Jax asked, twisting around in his seat in the front row and craning his neck to see over the sea of faces behind them.

"I have no idea," Tana said, realizing for the first time that she hadn't seen Julie at all except for a brief meeting in the inn's hallway a few hours ago. For most of the day, she and her team of helpers had been at the beach, setting up and finalizing the wedding preparations, and by the time they returned to the inn for a quick shower and to ready themselves for the ceremony, all thoughts of her mother had slipped from Tana's mind. She joined her brother in searching the crowd, returning smiles and waves to the guests who greeted her; most of the island's residents were accumulated on the beach at this point, and beside the canopy, the string quartet Edie had hired were readying their instruments.

Her search unsuccessful, Tana turned back

around, chewing her lip with worry as she said to Jax, "Do you think she's okay?"

"I'm sure she's fine," Jax said dismissively. "Julie does what Julie wants to do—she'll turn up eventually."

Tana opened her mouth to respond, but was stopped when Emery, seated on her other side, pointed excitedly at the canopy. "Look! It's starting."

Indeed, the minister had taken his place beneath the canopy, and the musicians, taking his cue, picked up their instruments. Soon, the delicate notes of Pachelbel's "Canon in D" floated into the air, and Tana's eyes welled up with tears the moment she caught sight of her uncle, who was now standing beside the minister. His hands were folded in front of him, and he looked dapper in his suit and tie; rather than the nerves Tana had been expecting, Henry seemed completely at ease, his face serene as he kept his gaze trained on the aisle, waiting for Edie to arrive.

The crowd turned as Edie's daughters walked down the aisle, looking beautiful in long, flowing pink dresses. Their own daughters, Edie's granddaughters, trailed behind them, holding baskets of rose petals that they strewed around them as they made their way toward the canopy. The little girls wore crowns of white roses in their hair, and Tana smiled at them as they passed, reaching back to squeeze Emery's hand.

The guests rose to their feet as one as the music paused before the song Edie had chosen for her walk down the aisle lifted into the sea breeze. Tana closed her eyes for a brief moment and listened to the beautiful notes of "Somewhere Over the Rainbow," allowing herself to be lost in the melody, before a soft gasp rippled through the crowd. She opened her eyes to see a radiant Edie at the end of the aisle, accompanied by Reed, who looked so handsome in his suit that it nearly took Tana's breath away.

Edie's dress was stunning, and it trailed behind her as she and her son began their slow walk up the aisle. More than one of the guests dabbed at their eyes as she walked past, but Tana let the tears flow freely, especially when she turned briefly and saw the look of absolute love and devotion on her uncle's face as he locked eyes with the woman who had stolen his heart.

Edie beamed at him, her face glowing in the sunlight streaming down on her as she and Reed stopped a few feet from Henry. Her son kissed her gently on the cheek, then held her hand for a brief moment as he whispered something in her ear.

Their eyes met one last time, and then Reed stepped away, taking his place at Henry's side as his best man as he and Edie turned to face each other.

"This is too much," Emery whispered beside Tana, her voice croaky, as Jax stood on her other side, smiling softly as he watched the couple. She thought she detected a hint of sadness in his expression as well, but she didn't have time to dwell on it, for at that moment, the minister began to speak, welcoming the guests and offering his congratulations to the couple, who were now staring deeply into each other's eyes, the rest of the world lost to them.

The seagulls soared overhead and the waves lapped gently against the shore as the ceremony got underway beneath a sparkling sky. Edie's gown billowed softly in the wind as she and Henry held hands, and before long, it was time for them to promise themselves to each other before everyone they knew and loved.

They had chosen to use the traditional vows, the ones whispered by the countless couples who had come before them, a celebration of love through the ages. Edie's voice was strong and clear as she spoke her promises to Henry, vowing to love him through the good times and the bad, for the rest of her life.

When it was Henry's turn, he faltered, opening his mouth to speak and then closing it again and shaking his head. He pulled out a handkerchief and pressed it against each eye for a brief moment, then tucked it back inside the pocket of his suit with a trembling hand, the other still clinging to Edie's.

But when he finally began to speak, his voice, too, was strong, his eyes never leaving Edie's face as he finished with, "I love you, my beautiful girl," the pure emotion in his voice leaving not a single dry eye on the beach.

And when he slipped the ring on her finger moments later, the cheer that went up from the crowd could surely be heard all the way back on the mainland.

"Daphne, this cake is exquisite," Reed said, sliding into the seat beside Tana.

"Isn't that your third piece?" Daphne teased, raising one eyebrow at him while Tana laughed. "Keep it up and there won't be enough for anyone else."

"Then they can stop by your bakery and buy a slice for themselves," Reed said around a mouthful of cake, giving her a cheeky grin. "See how helpful I am? I'm sending plenty of new business your way."

He offered the fork to Tana, who declined with a shake of her head as she cast her eyes around the partygoers. After a beautiful and heartwarming ceremony, followed by a romantic first dance where the newlyweds held each other close and Henry made good on his vow to leave his cane behind, the reception was now in full swing.

The open-air tents were filled with laughter and conversation as the sun drifted lower, casting its rays across the coral-streaked sky. Dinner was over and the party was ramping up, and Reed chuckled as he watched Emery and Jax tearing it up on the dance floor, doing some blend of the robot and the chicken that had other guests giving them a wide berth.

Daphne looked on, her eyes on Jax, her expression wistful, but Tana was barely paying any attention to her surroundings—she was too busy alternating between checking her phone and then the crowd for her mother, who still hadn't made an appearance. Tana had reached her by phone at the end of the ceremony, and an apologetic Julie had promised that she was running late and was on her way, but since then, radio silence.

Jax, catching sight of Tana's worried expression

as he took a break from the dancing and stopped back at their table with a glass of water and a plate of cake, shook his head and said, "You're going to miss the party, sis. I told you—stop worrying about Mom. I guarantee she got a call about a tiger somewhere in Africa and is already on the plane, ready to track it down."

"No, she wouldn't do that," Tana insisted. "Not without seeing Uncle Henry first."

Her brother's face softened. "You give her too much credit," he said, his eyes pained. "You'll be much happier when you realize that." Then the band struck up a slow song, and he turned to Daphne. "May I?" he asked. "For old time's sake."

Daphne hesitated, her eyes wandering onto the dance floor before meeting Jax's gaze. She glanced down at his outstretched hand, then set down her napkin and slipped her hand into his, allowing him to pull her to her feet. As they threaded their way through the crowd, Tana watched them, a feeling of sadness washing over her despite the celebration going on around them. Jax would be leaving the island for good in a few short days, and she couldn't help but feel that this missed opportunity between the two of them would haunt them for years to come.

Love was a precious gift, she thought, watching Henry and Edie in the middle of the dance floor, holding each other close, his hands steady on her waist, her fingers playing along the back of his hair. Then her gaze turned to Reed and she was startled to see that he was looking back at her, his expression intense.

"Have I told you how stunning you look tonight?" he whispered, leaning in close to her, his breath tickling her ear. Then he stood and offered her his arm. "Dance with me, and make me the luckiest guy in the room tonight."

Tana hesitated, casting one last glance around the tent, searching for her mother's face. Just as she was debating whether to slip away to the inn to check on her, her phone buzzed on the table, lighting up with a text message. She grabbed it and flicked up on the display, leaning in close to see in the dim lighting, her heart rate quickening when she saw her mother's name.

Got a call from a photographer buddy in Yellowstone. He finally tracked down those wolverines. It's a once-in-a-lifetime opportunity. At the airport now, heading out. Give Uncle Henry my love. XOXO.

"Everything okay?" Reed asked, frowning down at her.

Tana stared at the message once more, and then out at the dance floor, where Edie and Henry—and now Daphne and Jax—were holding each other close as they swayed in time to the melody. Emery was nearby, flirting with the twenty-something bartender, and Luke was standing in the middle of a crowd of Dolphin Bay residents, laughing and chatting and looking at ease as he sipped from his glass of wine.

And the most handsome man in the tent was beside Tana, looking at her with love and concern.

She wasn't going to miss out on another moment of this evening. She was going to enjoy it to the fullest.

"Everything's fine," she said, sliding the phone into her purse and stuffing it under the table. Then she stood and took Reed's hand. "Now come on. You and I are going to dance the night away."

And so they did.

EPILOGUE

The sky was darkening to a deep purple as Daphne locked the bakery's front door and slid the key into her pocket. It had been another busy day, another day to be thankful for all that had happened in her life over the past few months, but a sad day as well, a reminder of all that she had lost.

The island's sidewalks were nearly empty as she turned and strode down them, glancing alternately at her watch and the dark, rippling ocean off the harbor. As the ferry's lights turned on in the distance and she saw it glide slowly out of the dock, beginning its journey across the sea, Daphne picked up her pace until she was practically jogging, her eyes never leaving the water.

He'd asked her to see him off.

She hadn't been able to bring herself to say yes, and the hurt in his eyes, the sorrow, had been almost too much for her to bear.

But this… this was her way of saying farewell.

The harbor was silent as she reached it, stopping for just a moment to catch her breath before picking her way along the weathered wooden boards of the dock, careful not to slip in any of the pools of seawater that slapped over the surface whenever a large wave rolled in. The ferry was a pinprick now, a line of lights in the distance, and even though she knew he would never see her, she raised her hand, stretching it over the water, watching—for the second time—as the man she'd loved since childhood left the island.

"Goodbye, Jax," she whispered into the wind, pulling her sweater tighter around her body, hugging herself as much to ward off the chill as to comfort herself. Then she stood, still and silent, her eyes on the ferry until it finally disappeared, its lights fading into the night.

Only then did she turn and walk away.

DEAR READERS,

Thank you so much for reading **The Vow**, the fifth book in the Dolphin Bay series. I hope that you enjoyed it, and that you will join me for the story's conclusion in **Christmas at Dolphin Bay**, the final book in the series. Grab your copy now!

To be the first to know about new releases, sign up for my email list. I'll never share your information with anyone.

To stay connected, check out my Facebook page, send me an email at miakentromance@gmail.com, or visit my website at www.miakent.com. I love to hear from my readers!

And to help indie authors like me continue bringing you the stories you love, please consider leaving a review of this book on the retailer of your choice.

Thank you so much for your support!

Love,

Mia

Mia Kent is the author of clean, contemporary women's fiction and small-town romance. She writes heartfelt stories about love, friendship, happily ever after, and the importance of staying true to yourself.

She's been married for over a decade to her high school sweetheart, and when she isn't working on her next book, she's chasing around a toddler, crawling after an infant, and hiding from an eighty-pound tornado of dog love. Frankly, it's a wonder she writes at all.

To learn more about Mia's books, to sign up for her email list, or to send her a message, visit her website at www.miakent.com.

Printed in Great Britain
by Amazon